Speck of the Stars

Henry Boffin is an award-winning screenwriter and director, as well as a teacher and co-founder of the Australian production company Humdrum Comedy. His short films have won awards around the world and his first SF feature film is currently in development.

Speck of the Stars is Henry's debut novel.

*To Mum & Dad, for encouraging me to
forever have my head in the clouds — HB*

Speck of the Stars

Book One of
The Starfall Saga

Henry Boffin

FORD ST

First published by Ford Street Publishing
Melbourne, Victoria, Australia

2 4 6 8 10 9 7 5 3 1

© Henry Boffin 2022

This publication is copyright. Apart from any use
as permitted under the Copyright Act 1968, no part
may be reproduced by any process without prior written
permission from the publisher. Requests and enquiries
concerning reproduction should be addressed to
Ford Street Publishing Pty Ltd,
162 Hoddle Street, Abbotsford, Vic 3067, Australia

Ford Street website: www.fordstreetpublishing.com

First published 2022

A catalogue record for this
book is available from the
National Library of Australia

ISBN: 9781922696106 (paperback)

Cover illustration: Tomislav Tikulin
Printed in Australia by McPherson's Printing Group

Contents

A Quick Note on the Galaxy		1
1:	The Night Eaters	3
2:	The Study of the High Librarian	18
3:	Giddius Monk	31
4:	Tears in the Night	45
5:	The Galactic Imperators	61
6:	The Gumu Warren	77
7:	The Stranded Pirates	92
8:	Cry of the Starchild	109
9:	Lost in the Mist	125
10:	The Shriekers	141
11:	Double Deception	155
12:	Secrets of the Lost Planet	167
13:	The Star Eater	183

14:	The Final Test	197
15:	Into the Storm	213
16:	The Curse of the Starchild	225
17:	Speck of the Stars	243

A Quick Note on the Galaxy

The Universe is truly mind-boggling. It is a ginormous place consisting mostly of empty space and barren rocks, yes, but despite this, it is also teeming with life – if you know where to look. A huge number of living beings exist throughout the many galaxies that make up the Universe. From the humble human – just like you, dear reader – to the frighteningly hideous stinkrats of Glunderon. From the resourceful scavenger tribes of Gutterlings to the imposing gladiators of the planet Thrakkush, all races exist in a melting pot, ruled over by various kings, queens, emperors, empresses, titans, warlords, conquerors, and other rulers of a thousand different titles. In fact, there are so many races in just our Galaxy that, once upon a time, someone thought it might be a good idea to try and learn about them all. That someone was a member of one of the oldest and wisest of all the races in the known Galaxy: the Keepers.

The Keepers are famously avid historians, but after growing tired of researching the history of their own planet they found a new purpose: to begin the daunting task of logging the histories of every known being in the Galaxy. No small feat, of course.

This noble alien race soon realised that they'd bitten off quite a bit more than they could chew, and their home planet simply wasn't large enough to store such a vast amount of knowledge. So the Keepers decided that their only course of action was to build a spectacular spaceship; a satellite that would orbit their home planet of Varillis and become a seat of learning in which the entire history of the Galaxy could be stored. They named this magnificent satellite the Grand Orbital Library.

Nowadays, thousands of visitors come to enjoy the vast knowledge and fantastic stories contained within the walls of the Grand Orbital Library. These stories are as numerous as the stars that dot the night sky, and in this book is just one of those tales. Curiously enough, this particular story begins in the Grand Orbital Library itself, with a young human boy and his robot brother on their way to spy on a most monumental event. Little did they know that this one act would be the gateway to something much larger than either of them. Almost larger than the Galaxy.

Almost ... after all, it is very large.

1

The Night Eaters

'Wait up, Speck!' cried the droid as the boy in the grey jumpsuit hurtled down one of the many thousands of utility ducts within the Grand Orbital Library. Behind him, Speck could hear the wheels of his brother squeaking in protest as the little robot struggled to keep up. A grin took over his face.

'Come on, U-T,' Speck urged, glancing over his shoulder. 'We'll miss them arriving if we don't hurry.'

'I know,' said his brother, 'but I wasn't designed to go this fast. I'll break a wheel.'

Speck's grin grew wider as he took a left down an even narrower duct, ducking to avoid the low ceiling. The sprawling utility ducts of the Library weren't exactly built with humans in mind. Hidden just above the main corridors of the Library, the confined secret passages were just the right size for the utility droids who kept the spaceship running. The droids could easily zoom all around the Library in a matter of hours, unobstructed by the many dithering librarians and knowledge-seekers who otherwise clogged the spaceship's main corridors. Speck, on the other hand, had been forced to learn how to manoeuvre through the twisting miles of tight spaces. Despite his size, the Library's ducts were his home. He knew all the cramped little passageways like the back of his hand. After all, he'd spent most of his life navigating them.

Speck came to a halt as the confined duct seemingly hit a dead end – except it wasn't a dead end at all. On the floor was the beginning of a track, which ran up the wall. It was here that U-T and other droids had the advantage over his non-mechanical body.

Speck felt a rush of exhilaration as he heard the squeaking wheels of his brother approaching. He quickly launched into action, beginning to climb a set of rungs that scaled the duct alongside the track. As he climbed, his brother latched onto the wall and casually followed him, wheels whirring.

'We could still turn back,' U-T said hopefully as they climbed. 'You know how much trouble we'll be in if M-T finds out what we're up to.' The voice that came from U-T's chassis sounded distinctly nervous and Speck understood why. It was only an hour before power-down time. U-T was meant to be getting his joints oiled ready for the next day's duties and Speck should have been doing the homework the librarians had set for him. The boys were breaking the rules by gallivanting through the ducts at this time of night. They'd had to lie to their mother, claiming that they had an important errand to complete. Of course, Speck had been the one to do the lying. Robots weren't so good at bending the truth.

'I know.' Speck was red-faced as he climbed, casting a rueful eye at the ease of his brother's ascent. 'But it's the Night Eaters! Don't you want to know why they're here?'

'No,' said U-T. If a robot could ever look surly, that's how his brother looked at that very moment. 'We're not meant to be intrigued by our visitors, Speck, you know that. We make sure everything works the way it's supposed to and that's that.'

'Well, I heard the High Librarian say that the Night Eaters found something miraculous in the deep reaches of space – and they're bringing it here so they can research it!' Speck could hardly keep his voice down with the anticipation bubbling up within him.

'Sounds dangerous,' muttered U-T.

Speck rolled his eyes. 'Sounds exciting! Just help me out this once and I promise no more adventures for the next month, okay?'

U-T sighed and Speck almost laughed. In the years he'd known U-T the bot had taken on more and more human traits. He knew it was something their mother-bot would surely disapprove of.

'All right,' said the little bot, giving in. 'As long as

we're back before power-down.'

'We will be,' promised Speck, and the pair finally made it to the top of the climb. The duct levelled out and Speck knew that they would now be positioned high above the vast arrival hangar, where visitors' ships would dock and the Library's newest guests, the legendary Guild of Night Eaters, would be arriving at any minute.

Speck was excited. The Library received guests all the time, naturally, but they were usually just fusty academics or boring researchers. This, on the other hand, was one of the most famous bands of adventurers of all time, idolised by every child throughout the known systems. Speck had always dreamed of catching a glimpse of the Guild of Night Eaters. The Guild were explorers first and foremost, travelling to the most dangerous and exotic corners of the discovered Universe. To eat away at shadows of ignorance was their motto, and it was a motto Speck often murmured over and over while lying awake at night. Not once had Speck imagined he'd see one Night Eater, let alone the entire Guild!

A grate sat in the floor of the duct a few metres ahead of the pair, through which Speck could see the vastness of the arrival hangar. With trembling fingers, he swung his leather utility bag round his waist and sought out his screwdriver, fumbling with the tool in his exhilaration.

'Here, let me,' said U-T and the robot rolled

forward. A small socket on the front of the bot's chassis popped open and a screwdriver protruded forward with absolute precision. With it, U-T quickly made light work of the clamps holding the grate in place.

Together they pulled the grate in and placed it to one side.

'Oh no! We're too late!' Speck cried as he peered down below. The hangar was empty and the Guild's mighty flagship, the *Pilgrim*, sat quietly in its dock.

'No, we're not,' said U-T. 'Look. Here they come.'

Speck could see that the droid was right. The ship's embarkment ramp had yet to descend and at that very moment a procession of the Library's custodians, the wise Keepers, were filing into the hangar. Adorned in long cloaks that draped to their feet, the Keepers almost seemed to float as they entered at their usual leisurely pace. Each was at least three times the height of Speck with purple skin, small, squinting eyes and thick sprouts of white hair on their faces. Even the female Keepers had an abundance of whiskers on their cheeks and bulbously large noses.

At the head of the procession marched the High Librarian himself, Vargel Pren; the most prestigious of all the Keepers who lived on the Library satellite. It was the High Librarian who had first discovered Speck as a baby, all those years ago, abandoned in a spaceport in the middle of nowhere. Vargel Pren had decided to take Speck in and allow him to live aboard the Grand Orbital Library under the care of the droids. The High Librarian was tall, even by the standards of the Keepers. His face was forested by bristling white hair with only small areas of mottled purple skin peeking through the follicles. He wore spectacles above his crooked nose, behind which two small eyes darted inquiringly, as if ever hungry to seek out new knowledge.

The Keepers continued to file through the hangar and, to Speck's frustration, came to a halt on a raised platform just out of sight from his own viewing grate.

'No!' Speck protested in anguish. 'Not there!' He looked to his brother's questioning gaze. 'You'll have to lower me down, U-T. Just a little, so I can see.'

The little bot reversed slightly. This was U-T's way of showing his surprise.

'No, Speck, wait. I haven't had my winch serviced in months.'

'And whose fault is that? Come on. I don't weigh that much.'

U-T conceded that point and popped open another port on his chassis. A hook dangled out and Speck grabbed it, unspooling the attached wire and clipping it to his belt.

'Quick!' Speck hissed. 'The Guild are coming!'

And so they were. The *Pilgrim*'s ramp had finally lowered and the first of the Guild members were disembarking.

'All right. Just take it slowly,' said U-T.

Speck tried his best to comply, hanging himself from the open grate with as much restraint as possible. He felt U-T's winch lock, taking his weight. The wire attached to the hook went taut and U-T engaged his magnetic clamps, his body fastening securely to the floor of the duct. Slowly, the bot began to ease Speck down until the boy was hanging, suspended in mid-air, with an uninterrupted view of the entire dock. He was just in time.

Speck almost gasped as he saw the first of the Guild members marching out from the ship with ordered practice. They came in a multitude of different shapes and sizes. Unlike the Keepers, the Guild was made up of all different races of the Galaxy. Despite this fact they shared a common uniform: a crimson cloak that covered their figures from head to toe. They wore thick boots, gloves, and fearsome masks, so no part of their skin was visible. The masks were the only part of the uniform that differed from member to member. Speck recalled reading once that they were constructed from prizes won from the many exotic planets the Guild members had explored. Attached to them all were a medley of colourful feathers, jutting bones, intricate carvings, and twisted visages of otherworldly creatures.

At the front of the procession was a figure Speck recognised immediately. It was Giddius Monk, the leader of the Night Eaters and a human just like Speck. He wore the same attire as the rest of his Guild, but his cloak was decorated with gold trimmings. His mask was unmistakable, beautiful, and terrifying in equal measure – it was carved from a black, shimmering material and ringed with blood red feathers. A stony face was etched onto its surface with two glimmering sapphires set where the eyes would have been. As Giddius marched before his Guild members, his boots echoed with resounding authority. He reached the High Librarian and fell gracefully to one knee, the rest of the Guild fanning out respectfully behind him.

Speck's mouth was dry with anticipation.

'Humble leader of the Night Eaters,' spoke Vargel Pren in a booming voice that echoed round the hangar. 'The presence of your mighty Guild is most welcome here.' The High Librarian's eyes twitched and darted in their bird-like manner as he spoke and Speck suddenly felt exposed where he was hanging, sure that he would be seen at any moment.

Giddius Monk responded, but his mask muffled the Guild leader's words and Speck could barely hear them.

'What is he saying?' U-T whispered from the duct above.

'I don't know,' said Speck. 'I need to go lower.'

'We shouldn't . . .'

'Please, U-T! I'm missing it!'

U-T sighed, and Speck heard the whirring of the bot's winch as he began to descend lower into the gargantuan hangar.

'We have prepared for your arrival,' continued Vargel from below, responding to Monk's words. 'We are prepared to assist your research in whatever way we can. Please make use of our facilities as a token of our friendship. But pray tell, what is this marvel your Guild has discovered from beyond the edges of our Galaxy?'

This is it! Speck thought excitedly.

Giddius Monk responded again, yet Speck still couldn't quite hear what he said.

'Lower!' Speck hissed up to U-T. 'I think they're about to bring it out!'

U-T's winch whined and groaned as he dangled Speck even lower.

Giddius Monk continued to talk and a gasp arose from the amassed crowd of Keepers. They stood in stunned silence as the fearsome leader of the Guild gestured towards the *Pilgrim*'s ramp.

'I thought such a being was merely a legend,' Speck heard Vargel Pren say in awe.

The High Librarian is the most learned being in the Galaxy, thought Speck. What could ever shock him?

And from the *Pilgrim*'s ramp came four more Guild members, comprising musclebound aliens with towering frames. Between them they pushed a glass box that hovered above the ground. The box was filled with an opaque orange light.

'Behold!' sang Giddius Monk and it was the first of the Guild leader's words that Speck had been able to hear. Speck squinted at the glass box as it floated up the hanger.

'What is it?' asked U-T from the duct above.

In spite of his awe, Speck had to grin. 'I thought droids weren't meant to be intrigued by their visitors?' he teased. The bot fell silent above and Speck could imagine him sulking. But it wasn't like he could answer his brother's question even if he wanted to. The light that shrouded the glass box made it impossible to see what was inside.

'Ah, a stasis prison,' mused Vargel Pren far below. 'It pleases us to see you using such precautions whilst within our facilities.'

Speck frowned. A stasis prison? He'd read about those before. They were used to literally freeze a being in time. It was the most secure way of transporting anything dangerous. But what could they have found that had to be transported so carefully? If only he could hear Giddius Monk's words. He yearned to get closer, cupping his ear as he wriggled on the end of the harness.

'And now we will . . .' began Vargel.

The winch creaked. There was a small ripping sound. Vargel paused in his speech, his eyes darting up to where Speck hung.

'Oh no,' U-T gasped from above. 'My winch –'

A snapping sound sang out sharply. Speck's eyes bulged and suddenly he was falling, his stomach lurching with a thousand butterflies.

'Speck!' shouted his brother from above. The wire

had snapped! The hangar whizzed past his vision. He was tumbling, over and over, the world spinning round him. Crimson cloaks flooded his vision as air whistled past his ears.

Then, just as the hanger floor was rushing up to meet him, his fall began to slow. His descent paused and his body was surrounded by an all-encompassing blue glow. Around him hovered several small drones that had taken up position as if from thin air. They had caught him in an anti-grav net just in time. The drones gently lowered Speck's floating body to the ground and he landed with a soft thud.

When Speck looked around, all eyes were watching him. His blood ran cold. The terrifying masks of the Night Eaters surrounded him. Up on the raised platform, Vargel Pren peered down with a stony face. Giddius also watched the curious boy, the sapphire eyes on his mask twinkling jubilantly.

'It's comforting to see how well maintained the security is here,' said the leader of the Guild. A soft chuckle came from the rest of the Night Eaters and immediately two utility droids were at Speck's side, clasping at him with clawed hands and dragging him away. Filled with shame, Speck half stumbled, half slid along the hangar floor, watching as Giddius Monk turned back to Vargel Pren with an amused snort, already forgetting the spy who fell from the ceiling as if he was nothing more than a bothersome fly.

★

'What were you thinking?' fumed M-T later that night. Speck could clearly see that his mother-bot was agitated. Her wheels span relentlessly as she paced in tight circles. 'In front of our most prestigious guests and everything! Oh, what will they think of us?'

Speck could only look at the floor, embarrassed. It was well past power-down time in the utility droids' docking station that he called home, but he was certain that many of the bots situated around his raging mother were merely pretending to be on charge. Secretly they were listening to the news of the little almost-droid who had brought shame on the Library.

'I'm sorry, Mother-bot,' Speck said. 'I was just curious.'

'Curious?' cried M-T, flinging her arm attachments into the air. 'Why must you always be curious? And for what? A new tool or operating system, now that I would understand, but an unknown being brought in from the depths of space? What could that ever have to do with you?'

Speck shrugged. He knew his mother wasn't really angry. Robots didn't really feel anger, but he also knew that M-T had been uploaded with data on how to mother a human child. It was often hard to remember that her rage was just the result of program files she'd had installed into her hard drives.

Not that Speck knew what getting angry had to do with raising a child.

'Do you even understand why I'm angry?' his mother continued in response to his silence.

'Yes,' Speck murmured, 'because I embarrassed you.'

'It's not just that, Speck. I was worried about you, you silly boy. You could have been hurt!'

'But the security drones caught me,' argued Speck.

'You won't always have anti-grav nets there to catch you. Not only that – you broke your brother's winch too. Now he'll have to be repaired and miss out on two days of work!'

Speck sniffed bitterly. He thought he'd done U-T a favour by getting him time off from chores.

'You just don't think about others, do you?' said M-T, shaking her ocular system from side to side. 'And I've just heard that the High Librarian wants to see you tomorrow morning too.'

Speck swallowed. Vargel Pren wanted to see him? Misery fell on Speck's shoulders like a shroud.

'I'm sorry, Mother-bot,' he said again. This time he must have sounded like he meant it, for M-T stopped pacing in her tight circles and instead put a clawed hand on Speck's shoulder.

'Oh, Speck. I know it's in your nature to be different, but you must remember, you're my son and that makes you a droid. You've got to start acting like one.'

'But I'm not a droid,' said Speck.

'Well, maybe you are a human physically, but fate has made you one of us, you understand?'

Speck nodded sullenly. 'Yes, Mother-bot. I won't embarrass the Library again.'

'I know you won't, because for the next month you're grounded.'

'Grounded!' spluttered Speck. Looking at his mother's stony expression, he saw it was no joke. There was no point arguing with a robot. They never changed their minds.

'Now, we'd all better get some rest,' said M-T. 'I'm going to have to spend tomorrow on low battery mode as it is.'

M-T squeezed Speck's arm comfortingly before reversing and wheeling across to her docking station. Speck turned and began to climb up to the small shelf upon which his bunk bed was situated. Naturally he couldn't power-down in the same way that other droids could. He had to lie down on a soft surface and wait for sleep to finally come to him. For this purpose, the bots had fitted a small storage shelf with a mattress and blanket for him. It was here, overlooking the vast yet peaceful docking station and the dozing utility bots, that Speck powered down. From his vantage point he could see out of the single porthole that was fitted into the wall.

Sometimes he could catch sight of the planet Varillis through that little window, the home of the

Keepers. While he loved fantasising about what it would be like down on the planet's surface, he much preferred looking out the other way at the depths of space. Tonight, the window showed that endless expanse, studded with twinkling stars. Oh, how he yearned to be an explorer like the members of the Night Eaters and travel to those unknown places, bringing wonder and awe to the many races of the Galaxy.

But that would never happen, he thought. He was an orphan first and a utility robot second, not exactly explorer material.

Speck didn't dream of bold exploration like he usually did that night, instead falling into a restless sleep darkened by the cloud of the coming day and the inevitable punishment he was to receive from the High Librarian.

2

The Study of the High Librarian

When Speck awoke the next morning, the docking station was all but empty. The utility bots only required a few hours to charge and were often awake well before Speck could manage to rouse himself from bed. The night duty bots were just returning as Speck dressed himself and climbed groggily down from his bunk. He wished the returning droids a good power-down as he stole through the docking bay.

'Good luck with the High Librarian,' one of them said chirpily as they hooked onto a charge point.

Speck nodded back glumly. He hadn't forgotten about his punishment. With a heavy heart he got dressed and set off to the kitchens to find some breakfast before his meeting with Vargel Pren.

That morning, the canteen was far busier than Speck had ever seen it before, mostly thanks to the crowds of Night Eaters sitting at the tables. Without their masks on Speck could see the Night Eaters were of many different alien races. They seemed a lot less sombre than the previous evening too – laughing, jeering, and boasting, all the while drawing in looks of vague irritation from the mild-mannered Keepers. The only Night Eater who hadn't removed his mask was Giddius Monk. The Guild leader stood at the far end of the room, surveying his underlings. His mask was still, cold and impenetrable, the dual sapphires glinting in the fluorescent lights.

Following the previous night's escapades, Speck decided that he didn't want the Night Eaters to recognise him, and so he ducked discreetly into the kitchen in search of scraps. He was surprised when he turned the corner and practically ran into U-T holding a large ceramic bowl and wearing a dirty apron.

'Watch where you're going!' growled the bot, before realising who it was he'd run into. 'Speck! What are you doing here?'

'Looking for breakfast,' Speck replied, massaging his growling stomach. 'But I could ask you the same thing.'

U-T held the mixing bowl awkwardly in his claws. He had swapped out his electric screwdriver attachment for a whisk, which he inelegantly plunged into the batter that filled the bowl.

'They didn't have the parts in the repair shop for my winch,' grumbled the little bot. 'They've sent off for them but in the meantime, I've been given kitchen duty.'

He energised his whisk, kicking it into frantic action and sending batter splattering out of the bowl and all over his apron-covered chassis.

'I hate kitchen work,' he said.

'I'm sorry.' Speck tried to contain his laughter. 'If I have a chance, I'll put in a word for you with the High Librarian when I see him.'

U-T was about to respond when the head chef, a large creature with a clacking beak-like mouth, spotted them talking.

'Oi! Stop distracting my cooks!' he yelled, grabbing hold of a rolling pin from a counter and brandishing it menacingly. 'Can't you see I've got enough on my plate with all these darned Night Eaters as it is?'

'I'll see you later,' Speck said in an apologetic tone to his brother, darting away from the approaching rolling pin.

Half an hour later, after sneaking some of the last pancakes from the canteen, Speck made his way down one of the Library's many corridors towards the High Librarian's study. As per usual the walkways were quiet. The Keepers abhorred loud noise and they weren't known for listening to music either. Instead, the pre-recorded sounds of wildlife from the planet Varillis played softly on hidden speakers.

Sometimes they'd play the distant sound of gentle birdsong, other times the many clicks and croaks of the creatures that filled the planet's swamps. Speck had never seen any of the creatures that exuded the calming noises that filled the Library. He could only look at the illustrations in the Library's many books and imagine what it would be like to actually meet one face-to-face.

Usually, Speck would fantasise about such encounters as he walked the corridors, allowing his feet to take him down the paths he already knew so well, but today was an exception. He was too nervous about his upcoming meeting and, besides, he had now been joined by a small floating drone that emitted an irritating high-pitch hum as it flew along beside him. It was a security drone, programmed to stop him from going anywhere he wasn't allowed to go. If he did try and escape, it would cover him with a well-placed anti-grav net and sweep him helplessly back to his docking station. Having such a constant reminder of being grounded only worked to sour Speck's mood.

The little drone wouldn't let him turn back either, instead ushering him towards Vargel Pren's study at the very top of the Library, far further than Speck usually travelled. Sooner than Speck would've liked, they reached the end of a long corridor where a polished wooden door gleamed in the dim light. He paused, wondering if he should knock.

'Come on in, Speck,' said a voice from beyond the door. Speck's eyes widened and he wondered how the High Librarian had known he was there, but then he remembered the little drone floating next to him, its lens focused on him at all times.

Speck sucked in a deep breath and flattened down his messy hair, trying to look as neat as possible for his audience with the High Librarian. He hadn't been to the ancient Keeper's study since Vargel Pren had found him when he was very little. Sometimes it seemed to Speck that despite the many years he'd lived on the Grand Orbital Library, the High Librarian had forgotten he even existed.

Speck opened the door with a creak of the wood and stepped inside. It was like walking into a dream. Speck remembered the interior of the study only hazily from his youth but now, as he looked about, the missing gaps all filled in like quicksand. A fire crackled away in the corner and Speck was bathed in its warmth. Vargel Pren himself stood before a large desk in the centre of the study, above which floated a fearsome hologram of a snake-like creature.

'You're late,' said the Keeper.

'I'm sorry, High Librarian.' Speck bowed his head slightly.

Vargel nodded, not taking his eyes away from the hologram on the desk and beckoning Speck closer with a spindly finger. Speck obeyed, warily observing the hologram. Even though it was just an image of projected light, the creature was a fearsome thing; the animal was long and fat with a formidable rock-like carapace covering its entire body. What looked like thick hair covered the creature's face and underside, and two dark, glowing eyes peeked out from its deep-set face.

'What is it?' asked Speck as he reached forward toward the hologram, as if he could touch it.

'An adult space wyrm,' said Vargel. 'A creature that makes its home in deep space. Would it alarm you if I told you that this object here is a planet?'

Speck followed where the High Librarian was pointing and was aghast when he saw that the planet was hardly the size of his balled fist, tiny compared to the slithering creature.

'It must be huge!' Speck cried.

'A leviathan,' agreed Vargel. 'Yet despite their gargantuan size we know next to nothing about them.'

'Why not?'

'First of all, they are very rare. No being has witnessed a living space wyrm in eons. Not even the Guild. And secondly, they possess a curious power that makes them extremely volatile. You see, these mysterious creatures can do something that at first glance seems like an impossibility.'

Speck was enthralled as he looked from the space wyrm to the High Librarian. 'What can they do?'

'It is said that a fully grown space wyrm is capable

of creating a black hole,' replied the High Librarian.

'A black hole?' Speck repeated, astounded. He'd read about black holes. When stars grew old, they became too heavy and collapsed in on themselves. They became so heavy that they pulled everything in around them too. If you came within a certain distance of a black hole there was nothing you could do but get sucked into it.

'Yes,' Vargel continued. 'Space wyrms feed on star matter, you see. When they're finished eating, the star becomes unstable and collapses in on itself, creating a black hole. Though, fortunately for us, it seems that they only need to feed once every hundred years or so.'

'But how do they not get sucked in themselves?' Speck asked.

'Ah,' said Vargel with a pleased grin. 'That is the question, isn't it? No one truly knows. Though it is said that the only reason space wyrms have mastery of the black hole is because they do not fear them. To fear a black hole is to fall prey to one.'

Something was pulling at Speck's mind. The wyrm was a creature from deep space . . .

'Is that what the Night Eaters have brought with them?' he asked excitedly. 'A space wyrm?' Then he felt immediately stupid for asking the question. Of course there hadn't been a giant space wyrm in that small glass box.

Vargel looked down on him with a stony face,

but the twitches of a smile pulled at the edges of his mouth.

'No, not a space wyrm,' said the High Librarian. 'The Guild have brought with them something potentially far more dangerous.'

More dangerous? Speck's eyes widened and he yearned to find out more, but at that moment Vargel clicked his fingers and the hologram disappeared. The High Librarian settled into a chair behind his desk and gestured for Speck to join him. Speck realised the time for learning was over and the time for his punishment had come.

He swallowed and shuffled his feet as he felt the High Librarian's piercing eyes on him. Vargel said nothing and Speck realised, after a moment, that the elderly Keeper was waiting for him to make the first move. The serious nature of the summons flooded back into his heart and he remembered that, for all he knew, he could be banished from the Library that very day.

'I apologise,' said Speck, his voice quavering slightly. 'I shouldn't have spied on the arrival of the Guild yesterday.'

Speck dared to glance up at the High Librarian and was surprised to see that the Keeper looked bemused.

'Apologise?' said Vargel. 'What on Varillis are you apologising for?'

Speck blinked, taken aback.

'For embarrassing you and the rest of the Library. Mother-bot said you'd be furious.'

Vargel Pren chuckled softly. 'You have a curious mind, Speck. Never apologise for that.'

Now Speck was truly taken aback. 'You mean you're not angry with me?'

'Most certainly not. You were intrigued by the Guild's arrival. I would be worried if you hadn't been. Besides, where would any of us be without a healthy dose of curiosity? Still floundering in the mud pools of our home planets I suspect.'

Speck felt relief flood him. He hadn't realised until that point how tense his whole body had been, his hands screwed into tight balls.

'But maybe drag along a friend with a stronger winch next time,' said the High Librarian with a mischievous twinkle in his eye. 'Your mother-bot is right to be concerned, but only with the tenacious way in which you apply your curiosity. She is worried about your safety, no doubt, like any good mother should be.'

'Yes, sir.'

Then Speck frowned. He was certain that he had been summoned to be punished. It had never crossed his mind that there might be another reason.

'If you don't mind me asking sir, why did you summon me?'

'The right question,' said Vargel approvingly. 'Always remember, Speck. Life isn't just about asking questions but asking the right questions.'

'Yes, sir.' Speck hoped that he sounded surer of what the High Librarian meant than he actually was.

'You were raised by robots,' continued the Keeper, 'but you are not a robot. Your path is, undoubtedly, very different from that of your mother and siblings.'

'But I am a droid, sir,' said Speck.

'Your mother and siblings will always be your family Speck, and if a utility bot is what you wish to be then that is what you are. But you need not be caged in by what you are told to be.'

Speck shook his head, trying to muddle through the High Librarian's words.

'But if I'm not a bot, then what am I?'

He could hardly be a human. He barely knew how to be! Maybe he could have been a Keeper if the High Librarian had willed it. But no, instead he had been handed over to the bots. And if he wasn't a bot or a human or a Keeper, then what was he?

An orphan, he thought to himself – a baby abandoned in a spaceport somewhere with parents who didn't want him. The thought hurt and he shut it out as quickly as he could.

'Do you know why I took you in when I first found you as a babe?' asked Vargel, as if he could hear Speck's very thoughts just by looking at him.

'Because you felt sorry for me,' Speck said glumly.

'Not at all. I took you in because I felt you had a purpose that was a mystery to me. Where you came from, I do not know, but I am also filled with great curiosity and I am deeply intrigued as to your purpose. I often wonder what you will become.'

'But I've already become a robot. What else could I be?'

'This is my exact point, Speck,' said the High Librarian. 'You can be whatever you wish to be.'

Speck almost laughed out loud at that and the High Librarian's face turned stony in the face of his mirth.

'I-I can't just be anything,' Speck spluttered. 'I'm not strong or particularly wise. I've not learnt to be anything but a bot and I'm not even particularly good at that.'

Vargel scrutinised Speck even harder and Speck had to look at the floor under the Librarian's intense glare.

'If I hadn't shown you the hologram of the space wyrm just now, would you have believed that there exists a creature that eats stars and turns them into black holes?'

Speck shook his head. 'I suppose not.'

'Then maybe anything *is* possible. Which brings me to why I summoned you today. I have a job for you. A job of great importance. The Guild of Night Eaters will be here for the foreseeable future and while they're here they will need assistance. Droids are wonderful servants, of course, but I think someone with natural curiosity would be a far more suitable assistant to our Night Eater friends, don't you?'

Speck couldn't believe what he was hearing.

'You want me to assist the Night Eaters, sir?'

'More than that,' said Vargel Pren. 'I want you to be the personal assistant to Giddius Monk.'

'Me?' squeaked Speck.

'Yes,' replied the High Librarian. 'The Library must accommodate the Guild's every wish and I think you would be more than suitable to assist Giddius. Besides, I think you've made quite the impression with the Guild already.'

'Yes, sir.' Speck felt his cheeks glow red with embarrassment from the events of the day before. But his embarrassment was soon eclipsed by excitement. He could hardly imagine it. Assisting his hero, Giddius Monk. This was like a dream come true!

'Then you think you can manage this task, Speck?'

'Yes!' he blurted, before remembering his manners. 'Thank you, sir. Thank you so much!'

This time Vargel did grin, showing a wide number of ragged yellowed teeth beneath his purple lips.

'Very good. Then your duty begins straight away. I believe you'll find Giddius in the laboratories on the research deck.'

Speck scrabbled to his feet, shook the High Librarian's hand and made for the great wooden door before stumbling to a sudden halt.

'Oh, sir, I almost forgot,' said Speck, turning back. The elderly Keeper looked up, adjusting the spectacles on the bridge of his large nose.

'My brother bot, U-T, is being made to do kitchen duty while his winch is broken. It wasn't his fault really. Is there anything you can do for him? I'm sure he can still be useful, even without his winch.'

The High Librarian gave a soft smile. 'You are a good child. Always looking out for those dear to you. I'm glad to see it.'

Vargel scratched his double chin as he considered the request. 'I'll see what I can do about your brother. Now go, don't keep Giddius waiting. But do remember, Speck, stay true to yourself. No matter what.'

The Keeper looked serious as he spoke the words and Speck had to laugh nervously despite himself.

'I will, sir. Thank you.'

Vargel nodded once more and Speck exited the study, emerging back out into the quiet corridors of the Grand Orbital Library. The young boy shook his head and wondered what other surprises the day might hold.

3

Giddius Monk

'Mother-bot! You'll never guess what happened!' Speck came bounding down the halls of the guest dormitories, causing the working utility droids to look up, startled, from their cleaning duties.

'Whatever is it now?' pondered M-T as the bot turned from the bed she was making and watched the gangly youth racing towards her.

'Calm yourself, little-bot,' she said with a mechanical tut as Speck arrived next to her, red-faced and spluttering. 'What would our esteemed guests say if they saw you making such a hullabaloo?'

'I'm sorry, Mother-bot,' mumbled Speck, looking more than a little ashamed. 'I was just excited. The High Librarian has asked me to be the personal assistant to Giddius Monk himself!'

M-T froze for the briefest of split-seconds, unable to compute her son's words.

'He asked you to assist the Guild leader? But that's hardly a punishment at all!'

'I don't think he wanted to punish me, Mother-bot,' Speck said. 'In fact, he said it was good how curious I was about our visitors.'

'He said what?!' M-T physically shook with artificial anger. 'I'll have to have a word with that good-for-nothing . . .' She then caught herself, remembering who it was she was speaking about.

'I mean,' she quickly corrected herself. 'I'm sure our esteemed High Librarian knows exactly what he is doing. He is the master after all.'

Speck grinned from ear to ear, enjoying his sudden turn in fortune, but M-T looked about as miserable as a robot possibly could.

'What is it, Mother-bot?' he asked gently. 'Aren't you happy for me?'

The droid would have sighed if she knew how. Instead, she rested a small clawed hand on Speck's shoulder. 'Of course I'm happy for you, little-bot. My joy circuits are in overdrive. It just seems that you're growing up so fast.'

Speck frowned, unsure as to why this would ever make his mother unhappy, but he said nothing and a light buzzing sound just behind his left ear reminded him why he had come to find his mother in the first place.

'Oh yes,' he stammered. 'The High Librarian told me I had to report to Giddius immediately, but this little drone won't let me go anywhere near the laboratories. It keeps stopping me with one of those blasted anti-grav nets.'

M-T chuckled to herself and spoke to the drone in binary, commanding it to allow Speck to go to the research deck. The drone bleeped and blooped back at her, as if it were arguing that it was only doing what it had been told to do in the first place.

'There,' she said after the drone grumpily accepted its new instructions. 'All done.' Speck thanked his mother, planting a quick kiss on the side of her ocular component.

'Be careful, little-bot,' she called out as he turned to leave. 'Those Night Eaters may look exciting but they're working on some very important things. The last thing they need is an over-excited bot ruining their good work.'

'I know that,' said Speck. 'But I'll be good. I won't let you or the High Librarian down, I promise!' And with that he charged off, making his way towards the research deck, the little drone whirring angrily behind him as it attempted to keep up.

Unfortunately, Speck's confidence was dashed as soon as he entered the research laboratories. The usually sterile labs were a flurry of activity – the likes of which he'd never seen before, with droids dashing to and fro past the many Night Eaters who were bent over research stations or frantically tapping away at computers. The poor droids were rushed off their wheels, delivering equations, specimens and even snacks to the Library's guests.

A wave of raised voices washed over Speck as he picked his way through the crimson-coated figures.

Night Eaters yelled results and garbled numbers that meant nothing to Speck. Having lived amongst the Keepers for so long he wasn't used to such a racket and he was hard pushed not to cover both ears with his hands. Speck was also terrified that at any moment one of them might turn and question what right he had to be there. Fortunately, though, none of them paid Speck much attention. Other than a few smirks and whispers of 'Look, it's that kid who fell from the ceiling,' he was all but ignored.

As he threaded his way through the lab, he slowly became entranced by the wonders the Night Eaters were researching. The laboratory's normally vacant preservation tubes had been filled with specimens of all shapes and sizes. In one tube was a tooth the size of Speck's whole forearm. Another held a long squid-like creature with thin ears that looked like wings, its many eyes staring out blankly at the world.

'I wouldn't look at that one for too long, kid,' said a voice behind Speck. He turned to find a formidable Guild member peering down at him. He had skin the colour of chalky bone and a single yellow eye on his forehead.

'Why not?' Speck asked.

'That's a thought-flayer from the Kovellian system. They're known for hypnotising their prey.'

Speck's mouth dropped open and the chalky-skinned Guildsman nodded sagely.

'And they don't eat your flesh,' he continued. 'Oh

no. They eat your thoughts. Once one of those has latched on there's no cure. And some say they can hypnotise you even after they die.'

Speck gasped and quickly glanced away from the preserved creature, fearing he might fall into a stupor at any moment. His blood was still running cold as the Night Eater roared with laughter.

'Skell!' the chalky Night Eater called to one of his fellow Guildsmen. 'You shoulda seen this gullible kid's face! Priceless!'

'What'd you tell him, Garnu?' laughed back the one called Skell, a thin, bony-looking Guild member with large tusks erupting from below her hooked nose.

'I told him the thought-flayer could hypnotise you even after it died. He looked so scared I thought he might faint!'

The pair exploded into rapturous laughter and Speck turned, cheeks glowing red with embarrassment.

'You think a thought-flayer is some kind of joke, do you?'

The sombre voice had come from behind Speck's back. The pair of Night Eaters fell into immediate silence and Speck turned to be greeted with the glowing twin sapphires set into the ceremonial mask of Giddius Monk. Speck couldn't tell how long the Guild leader had been observing them for.

'N-no sir, of course not,' stammered Garnu.

'I can tell that neither of you has ever had the misfortune to meet a thought-flayer before,' said the Guild leader calmly. 'Do you know how I know?'

The two Night Eaters could only shake their heads.

'Because if you had met one you wouldn't see fit to make light of such a nightmarish creature.'

'Yes, sir,' mumbled the one called Skell.

'You see, I have encountered a live thought-flayer,' Giddius continued, turning his head minutely to Speck. 'This very specimen, in fact. I took some of its tentacles as my prize.' He gestured toward the edges of his obsidian black mask where several slick tentacles protruded from behind the crimson feathers.

'The thing near drove me insane,' said Giddius, his deep voice laden with severity. 'Do you know what it feels like to have your thoughts flayed?'

Speck took a sharp intake of breath and shook his head, unable to make his mouth work.

'It is the purest form of agony I have ever experienced,' Giddius continued. 'Like needles being jammed deep into your skull. You need an unbreakable resolve to deal with such a creature. A resolve that, I fear, is lacking in this sorry lot.'

Speck swallowed and the two underling Night Eaters looked away, ashamed.

'I have resolve, sir,' said Speck, using almost all of his bravery to utter any words at all to the imposing masked man.

Giddius looked on him for a length of time and Speck could only imagine what the Guild leader was thinking. He had no way of telling whether beneath that mask his features were as stony as the ones Speck saw or whether the Night Eater was merely smirking at him behind that cold exterior.

'My mask scares you, does it not?' Giddius asked after some time.

Speck nodded slowly. He didn't lie often, a trait he'd picked up from his robot family. The Guild leader snorted softly at his honesty.

'You're right to fear it, boy. That is the very reason we Night Eaters wear these masks. So that we may face fear every day. So that we become immune to its numbing effects and our resolves strengthen until not even the depths of the most inhospitable planet can spark terror in our hearts. That is truly what it means to be a Night Eater.'

'I see, sir,' responded Speck, eyeing the many trinkets on Monk's mask and imagining what multitude of evil creatures the fearsome Guild leader had faced in his time.

'But if you are to assist me you should know who it is you work for, I suppose,' mused Giddius and, with that, the Guild leader reached up and took off the heavy, obsidian mask. Speck was surprised to find the face of a much younger man than he'd expected looking down at him. Monk's face was round and almost boyish with red, curly hair sprouting beneath the hood of his crimson cloak. His eyes were the only part of his face that betrayed his experience. Two hard-set jewels almost as blue as the sapphires he adorned his mask with.

'Is this the face you expected to find behind the mask of the fearless Giddius Monk?' asked the Guild leader, his eyebrow arching. Speck realised his expression must have given away his surprise.

'Certainly, sir,' he stumbled. 'I just thought you might be the same age as the High Librarian.'

Monk's thin mouth curled into an amused sneer.

'Yes. Quite. You see, I was prepared for this role from a young age. You might say I was born into greatness. I come from a long line of Night Eaters. My father was an expedition leader, and his father before him. What I'm trying to say is, it's in my blood to lead this vagabond group.'

'I see,' said Speck quietly, feeling a little jealous that he had no such lineage. This time, however, Giddius didn't pick up on his poorly concealed emotions. Either that or he chose to ignore them.

'Come, let us leave these two to their work,' said Giddius, turning and beckoning for Speck to follow.

'So,' murmured Giddius as he led Speck through the crowded laboratory. 'The High Librarian sends me a new assistant. How charitable of him.'

'My name's Speck, sir,' Speck offered.

'Speck the spy,' Giddius mocked. 'Speck who fell from the sky. It was quite the entrance you made the other night.'

'I'm sorry about that,' said Speck, struggling to

keep up with the Guild leader's long stride. 'I just wanted to know what it was you were bringing to the Library. Nobody said that I couldn't and I've heard really exciting things.'

'Ah,' murmured Giddius, casting a suspicious eye down at his companion. 'And what things have you heard?'

Speck thought for a minute that he might have said something he shouldn't have. He was always getting in trouble for saying the wrong things. 'You're always putting your wheel in it,' M-T had once told him.

'Just that it's a very dangerous creature from deep space,' said Speck, and then he decided to take a punt. He had one chance to impress the leader of the Night Eaters. 'And it's got something to do with black holes – maybe.'

Giddius stopped immediately and swivelled to look down on his new charge. His blue eyes pulsed with a vivid energy.

'Interesting.' His stare was intense. 'And where did you hear this?'

Speck swallowed, thinking immediately that he had indeed put his wheel in it. Was it possible to get the High Librarian in trouble? Surely not.

'Nowhere in particular,' Speck lied quickly. 'I was just reading about them the other day. They sound fascinating.'

Giddius Monk nodded minutely before letting out a coarse laugh.

'The High Librarian did say you were a curious

one. Curiosity should be rewarded. If you work hard, I don't see why you shouldn't be allowed to see the creature for yourself.'

'Really, sir?'

The Guild leader nodded and gestured towards the far side of the laboratory where an intimidating door was guarded by two equally intimidating Night Eaters. Both were armed with glowing laser spears and anti-grav guns.

'Beyond that door is, without doubt, the most dangerous being in the Galaxy,' said Giddius quietly. 'A *Starchild*. I caught it myself.'

'A Starchild?' Speck echoed. It didn't sound dangerous at all.

'Oh, don't be fooled by its name. It is no mere infant. It is only called so because it has been mothered by the cosmos itself, a spawn of the very blazing stars we look upon as we dream at night.'

Speck felt a chill run down his spine as he looked at the guarded door, curious and terrified in equal measure.

'The true danger of the creature, however, lies in its abilities. Abilities that, if wielded incorrectly, could wreak great havoc throughout the Galaxy. But in the right hands, Starchildren can be used to create a new era of peace and prosperity.'

'How did you catch it?' Speck asked in awe and Giddius looked down on him with an arched brow.

'Full of questions, aren't you?' he mused. 'I'm starting to think a little too many for a mere assistant.

Come. Let us go to my study and I'll give you my list of tasks.'

Giddius led Speck to his study, a room above the laboratory that looked out across the chaos below. The room itself was a maelstrom of mess. Books, scrolls and tablets were strewn across every conceivable surface and one could hardly make out the Guild leader's desk for the mountains of research sitting on it.

'Now where is it?' Giddius pored through the piled mounds. Speck positioned himself at the door, unsure of where to stand. Not that he was able to concentrate much on the study. His mind was still abuzz with thoughts of the Starchild. He wondered what such a powerful creature could ever look like. Giddius had said that they were born of the stars themselves. Did that mean a Starchild was made of fire? Speck found his excitement slowly building. As assistant to Giddius Monk he could only imagine the tasks he'd be given. Maybe he would have to feed the creature? Maybe the Night Eaters would even teach him how to partake in their research? His name might one day sit as a footnote in the history books that detailed Giddius' amazing life. The thought brought a shiver of anticipation buzzing up Speck's spine and he could hardly stay still as he waited in the corner of the messy study.

'A-ha!' Giddius cried, holding aloft a tablet. 'Here we are. Your jobs.'

He handed the tablet to the patiently waiting boy.

Speck took it and began to read the list that occupied the glowing screen.

Immediately his heart fell.

'But sir, this is all just . . .'

'Hmm?' Giddius looked up from an ancient textbook he had already become enthralled by.

'Well,' said Speck carefully. 'Collecting your laundry, dusting your study. This is all droid work.'

Giddius stared at him in confusion.

'Yes. You are a droid, are you not?'

'I mean, yes, but I don't think the High Librarian meant for me to just do droid work as your personal assistant.'

'He meant for you to do whatever it was I wished. You are my assistant after all.' Giddius cocked an eyebrow and returned to the musty tome he held in his hands. 'Why?' he murmured. 'Is this work too difficult for you?'

'Not at all. I just thought . . .' Speck stumbled on the words. 'I just thought I might be able to help with your research on the Starchild.'

There was silence for a moment, and then Giddius burst into laughter, guffawing loudly. Seeing Speck's deflated face, the Guild leader quickly composed himself, holding a hand to his mouth.

'I'm sorry, boy,' he said, but though the rest of his face had grown sombre, his eyes still sparkled with mirth. 'You don't just get to be a Night Eater because the High Librarian requests it.'

'Oh,' said Speck, his heart sinking even further.

'And if you have any ideas that you might become a Night Eater, then I'm sad to say you should put them to bed right this instant. One does not simply become a Guild member. One is born to be a Night Eater. You understand?'

Speck swallowed and nodded slowly.

'I'm sorry if you thought otherwise, young Speck,' continued Giddius. 'The High Librarian should never have put such an idea in your head. You're much better off staying where you are, don't you think?'

Speck nodded and mumbled, 'Yes, sir.'

Giddius gave him a thin-lipped smile and returned to the textbook in his hands.

'Now on your way, Speck from the sky. Let me know when you've completed that list. There are always more jobs I need completed.'

Speck bowed, then immediately felt silly. He'd never bowed to anyone before in his life, but he felt as though Giddius was so great he'd never have a chance of being his equal.

Giddius was right, he thought as he exited the study and made his way to collect the Guild leader's laundry. He was just a droid who wouldn't even know where to begin researching the mysterious Starchild.

He broke into a run, feeling the tears finally break and trickle down his cheeks. The High Librarian was wrong after all. He couldn't be whatever he wanted at all. He was Speck the droid. Speck the orphan. And that was all he would ever be for the rest of his life.

4

Tears in the Night

The rest of Speck's week was spent tirelessly serving the leader of the Night Eaters. He collected Giddius' laundry, did his ironing, and pressed his garments. He tidied the Guild leader's office, organising the many hundreds of books and translation tablets into alphabetical order. He fetched dinner, cleaned plates, sent messages, brought messages back and typed out even more messages when the Guild leader was too busy to pay the correspondents any heed.

Despite it all, the nature of the Guild's research remained a mystery to Speck. He had always thought that he was fairly knowledgeable. Part of M-T's human mothering protocol was to allow Speck to have an education that extended beyond a droid's duty and every day he was allowed four hours in the extensive chambers of the Library to seek out knowledge by himself. But what he had learnt seemed of little use. The books he was tasked with finding for Giddius might as well have been blank for all the sense he could make of them.

By the end of the week, Speck was as ignorant of what the Starchild was as he had been at the start, and he was more exhausted than he could ever remember being before. He could hardly conceal his glee when Giddius Monk announced that the Night Eaters would be allowed a day off from their work to rest and recuperate. Speck's excitement was only marred when the Guild leader informed him that he himself would never dream of taking a day off, and he still expected Speck to serve his breakfast at six o' clock sharp. Speck bowed, drooping with fatigue, and started making his way back to the docking station.

It was well past power-down when he arrived home and the night-shift workers had already left for their nocturnal duties. Speck climbed up to his bed with aching joints and felt his body singing with gratitude as he lay on his mattress, and the welcoming nothingness of sleep washed over him like a thick wave.

He awoke later that night with a start. Blinking a few times, he waited for his eyes to adjust to the dark. Sweat adorned his brow. He'd been having a horrible dream where he was assisting the Night Eaters with their research, except he couldn't get anything right. He kept stumbling and falling when asked to take precious beakers of chemicals to a different lab and they'd slip right out of his hands, smashing on the ground. And every time the Night Eaters would laugh at his failure, splitting their sides with joy. It was always the chalky-skinned Garnu or Skell who were laughing. Or, more often than not, Giddius Monk himself, sapphire eyes twinkling with mirth.

Speck groaned. He didn't want to be Giddius Monk's assistant anymore. He was better off just doing the work he'd always done. His utility bot work was familiar and safe. He could joke around with U-T, play games when he got bored and, most important of all, not make a fool of himself.

Sighing, Speck rolled onto his side, looking down at the vast number of utility droids all silently docked. Their charging lights blinked in the dark like a thousand eyes. He wished he could power-down as easily as them. For a droid, sleeping was as easy as flicking a switch. No troubled dreams. Just rest.

There was no sound in the docking bay but for the gentle hum of the batteries doing their work and the electricity flowing into the robots. As Speck lay on his side, he realised that another noise was becoming faintly audible beneath them all.

Speck sat up, frowning. He wasn't imagining things. It was faint but the peculiar sound was there.

What was it?

Speck cocked his head. The noise was coming from the grating near his head. Curiosity piqued, Speck knelt, pressing his head to the grating and closing his eyes.

Yes, he could hear it now. It was a mournful noise, and it took Speck a moment to realise it was the echoing sound of distant crying.

Speck hadn't heard crying much. The robots never wept and he'd never witnessed any of the Keepers shed a tear. Speck seemed to be the only one on board the Library who was even capable of crying. And when he did, the bots would look at him with troubled confusion, unsure of the purpose of such an act.

'What function does this serve?' U-T had questioned him one time, after he had sobbed for hours on end after stubbing his toe. 'You're losing valuable moisture. I can't fathom how this works as a repair protocol.'

'He would do it all the time as a baby-bot,' said M-T. 'My downloaded research says it is designed to attract the protection of the human's mother.'

'But there are no human mothers around here,' said U-T in confusion, and they all agreed, Speck included, that they had no idea what it was all about.

Despite having only heard his own sobs before, Speck was sure it was the sound of crying that he was listening to as he pressed his ear firmly to the grate.

Was there another human child on board? he wondered. Was it one of the Night Eaters bawling their eyes out? Speck bit his lip as he sat in the dark. The crying continued and he soon realised he'd never be able to get back to sleep without investigating the source of the noise.

Climbing into his jumpsuit, Speck slipped his screwdriver out of his utility belt and made short work of the grating. He crawled into the opening and before long the duct opened out and became one of the many service ducts that ran through the entire Library. The crying was louder here, echoing down the duct. Speck plucked a head lamp from his belt to help illuminate the way. He managed another few metres before a familiar buzzing noise sounded near his ear and the glint of the little security drone's eye fell before his eyes.

'Oh, blast you,' Speck hissed at the little security drone. 'Give me a break, will you?'

The little drone floated away slightly, as if taken aback. It bleeped and blooped in its own digital language, sounding very defensive to Speck's ears.

'Please don't take me back,' Speck begged. 'I just want to find out what's making that sound. Nothing more. I won't get into trouble. I promise.'

The little drone shook from side to side and its little eye blinked red.

Speck sighed. 'Well then, I guess you'll just have to take me back if I go somewhere I'm not allowed.'

It gave a happy little bleep and fell into place next to Speck's head as he started down the service duct towards the crying.

'I should probably give you a name if you're always going to be by my side,' said Speck thoughtfully. 'What about Nuisance? I could call you Nuis for short.'

The little drone gave another happy little bleep and continued to hover alongside him.

Following the sound of the sobbing took longer than Speck could have imagined. The service ducts appeared to channel the noise over a great distance and after ten minutes of darting through the cramped passageways, he still hadn't discovered their source. He was constantly worried that at any moment the sound would cease and he'd be lost. Yet the sobbing seemed to show no signs of abating. The longer it went on the more curious he became as to who could be so miserable.

Despite their meandering path, the little drone Nuis had yet to snatch Speck in one of its anti-grav nets and drag him back to the docking station. He could only presume that he hadn't yet gone to a restricted part of the ship. As he scrabbled through the ducts, he began to suspect where it was he was being led and, before long, his suspicions were confirmed.

'The research deck,' Speck whispered as they stood before a gleaming service grate. No wonder the little drone hadn't snatched him away yet. His destination was somewhere he had been permitted to go, thank Varillis. He cast a nervous glance at Nuis just in case, but the bot merely continued to stare directly ahead, merrily unaware of any wrongdoing.

'Maybe I should go back?' Speck whispered to the little drone. The drone's eye flickered green to say,

'Yes, that would be a good idea.'

But the cries sounded so human. What if it needed help? And he was curious too. He wouldn't be able to sleep without knowing what was making that melancholy sound.

Where would any of us be without a healthy dose of curiosity? Vargel Pren had said.

'I'll just have a quick look and then I'll go straight back,' Speck told the drone. He took a deep breath and unhooked the screwdriver from his utility belt. Nuis' eye glowed red and the drone buzzed angrily near his ear as he opened the grate.

'I know what I'm doing,' Speck told the little bot. 'I'm just being curious.'

The grate opened and Speck dropped through before he had a chance to lose his nerve. The room beyond was a laboratory that he'd never been in before. It was much smaller than the one Giddius had shown Speck the day before. The chamber was very dark, lit only by the ambient glow of dimmed lights that ran along the corners. The light cast a flickering glow across the spotless room, starkly contrasting the mess that littered the larger laboratory.

The sound of crying was quieter now that he was in the actual laboratory. Straining his ears, Speck realised the sound was coming from a containment cell at the back of the room. He peered into the shadows but still couldn't make out whatever it was that was sobbing so miserably.

He'd have to get closer. He took a few steps forward, casting his head torch around – and froze.

There, only a metre away from him, was a Night Eater sentry. The Guildsman's mask was faced directly toward him and it had one hand curled round a laser spear. Speck's eyes widened and his breath halted in his throat. Surely it had seen him! But bizarrely, the Night Eater didn't move an inch. Speck frowned. Could it be that somehow he hadn't been spotted?

Then he realised that the guard wasn't standing at all but was instead perched on a stool. The Night Eater's chest was rising and falling in a gentle, constant rhythm and Speck could just hear soft snoring emitting from behind the mask.

The guard was asleep! Speck let out a deep breath.

Carefully, Speck picked his way past the guard and towards the research cell at the far end of the room. The cell only had three walls, with the open side being covered by a translucent laser field that stretched from end to end. Speck knew that touching its glittering surface would send a bolt of electricity sizzling through his body and he made sure to keep a wide berth as he peered into the darkness within.

Only the centre of the containment cell was illuminated. The corners of the little room were cloaked in shadows. In one of these corners Speck could just make out a tiny, huddled figure, shoulders heaving as its mournful cries sounded out.

Speck cleared his throat, as loudly as he dared.

'Hello?' he whispered.

The crying stopped for a moment – but only a moment. Beside Speck's head, Nuis was buzzing and bleeping in an agitated manner. Speck batted at the little bot with one hand.

'Excuse me. Are you all right?' Speck said, a little louder. This time the crying did stop, replaced instead with muffled sniffing.

'No,' came a fragile voice from within. 'Do I sound all right?'

Speck swallowed. He didn't know how to comfort a crying creature. After all, he'd never met any, other than himself. What made him feel better when he was sad?

His mother-bot, he supposed. Though he could hardly go and get M-T to comfort the imprisoned creature.

'Why are you crying?' Speck asked instead, edging a little closer to the containment field.

'I'm lost and scared and they won't let me leave,' came the wavering voice from within the cell. It sounded young and defenceless, but most of all it sounded scared.

Like a child, Speck thought suddenly, and his eyes widened.

'Are you the Starchild?' he stuttered.

The creature gave out a long sigh. 'That is what they call me. I do not know my real name, though.'

'Oh,' said Speck, his breath catching. Surely this wasn't the Starchild. Giddius had told him that it was the most dangerous creature in the Galaxy – a child only by name – but this scared, huddled creature didn't look that powerful, or dangerous. It just looked frightened.

'I lost my parents,' sobbed the creature quietly. 'And I can't remember where they are.'

'I'm sorry,' said Speck, suddenly feeling very guilty for being on the free side of the containment cell. 'I lost my parents too,' he added with what he hoped was a reassuring smile.

'Then you know how it feels?' asked the fragile voice from the cell. The creature finally looked up. Speck gasped as he saw its eyes, blazing out from the shadows like twin suns.

'I do,' said Speck, collecting himself.

The Starchild blinked.

'What is your name?' it asked.

'Speck.'

The Starchild considered this and nodded slowly, its tears finally abating. The tiny figure stood and, to Speck's surprise, began to hover away from the ground, levitating above the cell floor. Speck watched in awe as the creature floated forward, finally emerging from the shadows. Speck could see it clearly now. It was indeed a small and child-like figure, dressed in drab purple rags. Its tough, leathery skin had several deep cracks in it. From these cracks emerged the colour of deep space, pulsating with a velvet glow. Its hardened skin formed a natural hood over the top of its head, covering its face and allowing only its blisteringly intense eyes to be seen.

'Speck,' repeated the Starchild, as it floated forward. 'Your name is like a mote of stardust. Are you also made from the stars?'

'No,' mumbled Speck. 'I wish I was. It's just a name I got when I was young. I'm small compared to the Keepers, and I was really small when they found me – so they called me Speck.'

'I wasn't found,' said the Starchild glumly. 'I was stolen. They took me – the ones who hurt me – and all I can remember is pain.'

Speck bit his lip, deeply troubled. He looked towards the slumbering Night Eater at the far end of the laboratory. 'You don't look that dangerous to me.'

'I have a great power, it is true,' explained the small creature. 'But I am not dangerous. I did not even hurt them when they took me, even though they were so cruel.'

A tear of fire dribbled down the Starchild's cheek as it spoke. Its voice was on the verge of cracking.

'They don't want to hurt you,' Speck said quickly, though his words didn't sound confident. 'I think they just want to find out how you do – whatever it is you do.'

The Starchild scoffed, and for a moment its eyes blazed with anger.

'Then why do they keep me imprisoned? Why

did they take me away from my parents? And what do you suppose they'll do with me when they are finished with their "research"?'

Speck swallowed, recalling the many trophies that lined Giddius Monk's mask.

'The one with the cold eyes,' whispered the Starchild, as if reading Speck's mind. 'He is the worst. My ears are more sensitive than they think. I heard him talking to the others. He wants my eyes. He wants to replace the blue stones he wears with the brilliance of a thousand stars.'

With that, the Starchild crumpled onto the cell floor, its small frame heaving with fresh tears.

Speck didn't know what to say. He couldn't deny what the Starchild said. The Night Eaters were indeed bullies if they picked on this innocent creature so viciously. Hadn't Giddius said that it was just a child by name? Yet here it was: a scared, helpless little boy – like he was – alone in the Galaxy.

'I'm sorry, Starchild,' whispered Speck. 'I had no idea.'

'Of course you didn't,' sobbed the Starchild. 'They keep me hidden. They say I'm too dangerous to be seen, but all I want is to be free and to find my parents again.'

Speck exhaled slowly. He looked at the security panel that sat on the wall next to the containment field. It was secured by a password, but Speck was a utility droid. He could open it if he wanted. Speck always loved playing the game of 'bypass the security protocol' with U-T.

'Do you think I'm a monster?' asked the Starchild suddenly. Speck looked up. The little creature was levitating again.

'No,' said Speck.

'Then will you help me?'

Speck stuttered.

'I'd get in a lot of trouble,' he said quietly.

The Starchild nodded slowly. It slumped to the ground, accepting its fate.

'If I did help you,' Speck said slowly, picking his words carefully. 'Would you promise to leave straight away and not hurt anyone?'

'All I want is my parents.' The creature started crying again. 'I don't wish to harm anyone.'

Speck nodded, mind ticking. If he freed the Starchild, he could run back to bed before anyone knew about it. The Night Eaters would have lost their prize, but no one would be able to hurt it anymore.

What about Giddius? nagged a voice in Speck's head. What about your hero? Can you disappoint him?

But then Speck recalled the way Giddius had laughed at him earlier that week. The way the Guild leader's eyes had sparkled with mirth even as he tried to cover his guffaws of laughter.

With that, Speck made up his mind. Marching over to the security panel, he plucked two terminal connectors from his belt. Nuis saw immediately what he intended to do and bleeped sharply in alarm. Its sole eye turned red as it darted before Speck's face.

'Go away,' Speck hissed and batted the drone away. He was glad that Nuis wasn't allowed to use its anti-grav net on him. He was allowed to be here. He was meant to be here. Speck connected the terminal leads to the security panel and slid his control tablet out of his belt. Tapping on the screen of the tablet, he began working away at the security protocols. It wouldn't take long, but with Nuis barraging him the Night Eater guard might wake up before he was done.

'You promise you'll leave straight away?' Speck asked, pausing in the midst of his tapping and looking up at the Starchild.

'Speck, you have my word.'

Speck nodded and looked back down to his tablet screen.

'Then here goes,' he said, tongue stuck between his teeth as he concentrated.

'You are truly setting me free?' asked the Starchild softly, voice laden with hope.

Nuis gave up trying to stop Speck. It turned and glanced round the laboratory in alarm. Then, with a bleep of realisation, it swooped over to the sleeping Night Eater.

Oh no, Speck thought.

Nuis was bombarding the slumbering guard with

its shrillest sounds: a cacophony of beeps and binary code.

The guard stirred in his sleep.

'So close,' whispered Speck, tapping desperately at the tablet.

Then he was there. The screen of the console turned green as the security was cracked. The option came up on his tablet to shut down the containment field.

Nuis bleeped even louder. The Night Eater finally awoke with a start, mask slipping from the creature's face as it sat up, startled.

Speck tapped on the console. The containment field shut down.

'Thank you, Speck,' whispered the Starchild.

And then the world exploded.

Speck was yanked forward like a fish on a line, hurtling through the air into the containment cell, tumbling over and over. The Starchild was somehow suddenly outside of the cell in the laboratory, hovering in the air, eyes blazing with victory. The containment field reactivated and Speck realised too late that he had been tricked. He was trapped. The Starchild pointed at the wall of the laboratory and there was a huge, crackling spark of energy. The wall of the laboratory exploded and the metal of the spaceship peeled away like tin foil. Open space and glittering stars were clearly visible beyond it. Speck could only watch from the safety of the containment field as the cold vacuum of space began sucking oxygen out of the laboratory, pulling debris and research equipment along with it. In the midst of it all floated the Starchild, calmly levitating as it slowly made its way through the hole and out into the endless void of space.

'Thank you, Speck,' said the Starchild, and its voice was just as loud in Speck's head as it had been when he was only metres away. 'Thank you for being such a fool.'

And then the Starchild was gone. Speck was left all alone. The Library's alarms blared a deafening klaxon and red lights flashed erratically.

What on Varillis have I done? Speck thought miserably, tears bubbling in his eyes as he huddled in the corner of the containment cell.

What have I done?

5

The Galactic Imperators

M-T's wheels whined as she paced the corridor, shaking her ocular system every so often. Speck sat slumped to one side, head buried in his arms.

Everything had happened so fast. He still couldn't quite comprehend it. All he knew was that the Grand Orbital Library was now in a state of chaos and it was entirely his fault. Night Eaters and utility bots alike scooted by, occasionally casting him furious looks. Even the usually reserved Keepers moved with haste, glancing down at him with disapproving stares as they passed.

I've really done it now, Speck thought. If the High Librarian didn't kick me off the Library before, then he definitely will now.

M-T hadn't said anything as Speck sat there, awaiting his fate. He was certain she was delving deep into her human parenting programming and weighing up the different options of what to do with him.

Speck had cried for what felt like forever in the Starchild's cell, until the oxygen had finally finished roaring out of the lab and it became eerily calm. With no air, the gravity simulator had switched itself off, and Speck could only watch as loose debris floated serenely past his cell in the vacuum. It wasn't long before utility bots came pouring into the remains of the laboratory, ready to seal the hole that the Starchild had created. Once the horrific tear in the wall had been welded closed, the door to the lab slid open and the place was flooded with frantic Night Eaters. Accusing glances and venomous words fell on Speck, as he sat in the Starchild's containment cell with nowhere to hide.

Eventually they released him from the cell and no sooner was he free than M-T was at his side.

'Come,' she said simply. 'Let's go.'

Speck had swallowed down his excuses and followed her, head down. As they left, Speck spied the slumbering guard and Nuis being released from the containment cell next door and Speck felt a pinprick of relief that they had both been spared the terrible fate of being sucked out into space. The poor Night Eater looked almost as wretched as Speck felt.

They passed Giddius Monk on the way out too. Mask adorned, the Guild leader completely ignored Speck as he went by. He could only imagine the fearless explorer's face was not dissimilar from the look of fury already carved into his fearsome mask.

'I'm sorry,' Speck whispered to his mother's back as she led him out of the laboratories and down a corridor.

M-T didn't respond. She merely continued to take him away from the scene of his crime. A group of utility bots sped past the duo, all on their way to help remedy the gigantic mess he'd created. He looked for the face of U-T – any friendly face would do – but he saw only strange bots, staring at him openly with their ocular systems.

That's right, he thought. Here's Speck, humiliation of the Library.

'What will happen to me, Mother-bot?' Speck asked quietly, as his tears finally subsided. M-T paused in her tracks. She looked over at her son.

'I don't know,' she said finally. 'You've broken so many protocols. I don't even know where to begin.'

She looked down at the floor. Speck thought that she looked smaller than he'd ever seen her before.

'I'm so sorry, Mother-bot,' sighed Speck. 'I know you want to be a real human mother. I let you down.'

'I don't care about all of that, Speck!' cried the little bot with sudden outrage. 'I don't care whether you humiliate me, or the Library. I just want you to be safe! It just doesn't compute. Why would you do such a thing? You were centimetres away from being sucked out into space! Space!'

Speck felt a lump form in his throat. His tears threatened to return.

'And now this mess is so big that the Galactic Imperators are on their way,' murmured M-T.

'Who?' Speck asked, frowning.

'The Galactic Imperators,' said M-T. 'The Emperor's personal army, Speck. It's that serious!'

Speck groaned and buried his head into his hands. The Emperor was the most powerful being in the whole Galaxy. If he was involved then it must be serious.

'I was only being curious,' he said in a resigned voice. 'The High Librarian said it was good to be curious.'

'There's a difference between being curious and being reckless, little-bot. What you did put not just your own life in danger, but the lives of all of those on board. Who knows what that creature could have done after being freed? We're lucky the Library's still in one piece.'

Speck shuddered. He recalled the blazing eyes of the Starchild. He had trusted those eyes. He had thought the creature was just a scared child, longing for the embrace of a parent it had never known. Just like Speck.

It had known, said a voice deep inside him. It tricked you.

'Thank you for being such a fool.' That's what the Starchild had said.

And it had been right.

A little later, U-T came wheeling sheepishly along

the service duct, giving Speck a quick pitying glance with his ocular system.

'There you are, U-T,' said their mother, evidently relieved. 'Where have you been?'

'Sorry, Mother-bot. They had me helping to cook an early breakfast for our guests. The Night Eaters are demanding a good feed before setting out after the creature. And not just that. I bumped into this one on my way here.'

From behind U-T floated a rather sheepish looking Nuis. The little drone bleeped in a shy manner, eye glowing a mournful blue.

'You!' M-T hissed angrily at the little drone. 'Fat lot of good you are. You were meant to stop him from doing reckless things.'

The little drone bleeped defensively, as if trying to explain that it had tried its best to stop Speck.

'No excuses,' she snapped. 'I want you and U-T to take Speck back to the docking bay, you understand? All we can do now is wait to hear from the High Librarian.'

'Yes, mother,' said U-T sombrely. Nuis bleeped in a similarly resigned tone.

'Off with you,' M-T barked, before wheeling off down the corridor.

Speck sighed, slowly getting to his feet.

'I'm sorry, U-T,' he mumbled quietly to his robotic brother. 'I didn't mean to give you extra kitchen duty.'

'It's okay,' his brother said. 'At least the Night

Eaters will be leaving soon. We'll have far fewer mouths to feed tonight.'

Speck nodded. It was little consolation, but at least it was something.

'And I'm sorry, Nuis. I didn't mean to get you caught up in all this trouble.'

The little drone turned away, emitting a little bleep that sounded to Speck's ears like a particularly grumpy humph!

Speck sighed once more.

'I've really screwed up this time, haven't I?'

U-T couldn't seem to find the words to answer, which was unusual for a robot. Instead, he extended a clawed hand.

'Come on. Let's get you back to the docking station.'

The journey back felt longer than Speck ever remembered it being. As they travelled, the trio passed the arrival hangar and Speck recalled, with a lump in his throat, how excited he had been only two days prior. Back then, he had been jubilant to see the *Pilgrim* arriving and the resplendent Night Eaters emerge from their grand vessel.

The Night Eater's ship was no longer there. It seemed that the Guild had already set out after their quarry. In the *Pilgrim*'s place was a ginormous space carrier, which occupied the majority of the hangar. Compared to the *Pilgrim*'s sleek design, this new spaceship was absolutely hideous. Roughly oblong in shape and rust red in colour, the new ship was more a hulking piece of misshapen metal than a spacecraft.

'Whose ship is that?' Speck asked as they walked along a corridor that ran beside the hangar.

'That?' said U-T, looking through the perspex viewing window. 'That's one of the Galactic Imperators' ships.'

'The Imperators? They're already here?' Speck exclaimed. 'That was fast.'

'Oh yes,' U-T said matter-of-factly. 'They've been here for quite some time. The Imperator ships have the fastest light-speed engines in the Galaxy.'

Speck had to pause to marvel at the size of the craft. He'd never seen a ship so large that wasn't designed purely to orbit a planet – like the Library itself. Despite everything, he felt his curiosity bubbling up once more.

'Speck!' U-T hissed. 'We can't dawdle.'

Nuis bleeped in a despairing tone, as if to say, 'See? This is what I have to put up with.'

'One minute,' Speck said. 'I'm not putting anyone in danger just by looking, am I?'

U-T conceded the point and wheeled round to join Speck at the window. Beyond the perspex there was a flurry of activity. The ship's many entry ports were open and emerging from them were the Galactic Imperators themselves, barking orders and shuffling to and fro with military precision. Each one had dull, grey skin, a large muscular frame, tusks erupting from their snouts and four arms protruding, with which they grasped bulky laser rifles. Speck shuddered as he watched the highly disciplined soldiers. A single one would be a formidable opponent for even the most terrifying being. No wonder the Emperor of the entire Galaxy used them as his own private army.

Amidst the ordered chaos, smaller aliens scuttled across the ship's surface. They were long, thin creatures with oversized bat-like ears. These smaller beings seemed thoroughly preoccupied making hasty repairs to the spacecraft, welding away with lasers whilst being completely ignored by their hulking counterparts.

'Who are they?' Speck asked, pointing at the smaller creatures through the glass.

'I don't know,' said U-T. 'Hang on. I'll find out.'

U-T's ocular gaze became distant and Speck could tell the little droid was accessing the Library's vast network, downloading data on the Imperators and their ship.

'The Imperators don't use utility bots for maintenance,' the robot continued as he blinked out of his data trance. 'They use a race of beings called Gutterlings. Each of their ships contains a separate tribe that navigate and keep the ship running. The Imperators feed and build homes for the Gutterlings, and in return the Gutterlings keep their ships ticking over.'

'No utility droids?' Speck murmured as he

watched the spindly little beings at work. 'I thought utility droids were everywhere in the Galaxy.'

Suddenly a hoarse cry went out from one of the Imperators and an alarm began sounding in the hangar. The Gutterlings rushed to pack away their tools, disappearing within the craft through minuscule openings.

'That's the hangar door alarm,' explained U-T. 'Looks like they're heading out in search of the Starchild, too. Thank Varillis the Imperators aren't planning on staying for dinner. They look like they'd eat a deck-load of food each.'

Speck sighed. An idea was whirling in his head – a crazy idea which he worked quickly to dismiss. But no matter how he tried, it kept resurfacing, along with his mother's look of abject disappointment.

'It was my fault,' Speck said quietly. 'It was my fault and it's my responsibility.'

'What?' U-T replied. Nuis gave him a quizzical bleep.

'Mother-bot is always telling us that we should take responsibility for our actions, right?' Speck frowned.

'I suppose.' U-T stared at him. 'But I think she was referring to things like leaving a Librarian's cloak in the tumble dryer for too long.'

'This is my responsibility,' Speck said firmly.

U-T shook his head. 'What is wrong with you recently, Speck-bot? Enough of this. Let's go back home.'

U-T was already wheeling away. Nuis followed, humming merrily along, but Speck stayed where he was, watching as the last few of the Imperators made their way into the hulking ship.

It was such a large ship, he thought. Cavernous. It would be easy to get lost inside it. Or to hide in it.

The hangar door alarm continued to blare.

'You can be whatever you wish to be.' He heard the High Librarian's voice whispering in his head.

Speck began moving before he could lose his nerve, jogging towards the nearest door to the hangar.

'Speck!' came U-T's distressed voice from behind, but Speck ignored his brother-bot. He opened the sliding door and, staying low, darted across the hangar, diving behind a crate of cargo not more than fifty metres from the Imperators' ship. The last of the hulking beings were just ducking into the entry ports as the alarm's siren rose in intensity.

He made to run but – he was stuck on something! He looked down, alarmed, to find a panicking U-T tugging at his arm with a claw. Nuis was buzzing with alarm over his brother-bot's shoulder, eye glowing red.

'Speck! What the circuit-board are you doing? The hangar doors are going to open any second! You'll be sucked into space!'

Speck pulled away, but U-T's grasp was strong and he couldn't free himself from his brother's grasp.

'Let me go, U-T,' he pleaded. 'Please. I need to bring the Starchild back.'

'But you won't stand a chance out there, brother-bot!'

Speck glanced from his robotic brother to the Imperator's warship. Any moment now the ramps would disappear and his opportunity would be lost forever.

As he struggled to decide, he realised that U-T was hurriedly speaking to Nuis in binary: a lightning-fast succession of blips and bleeps.

'What are you telling it?' Speck demanded.

'I'm giving it permission to use its anti-grav net on you so we can take you back to the docking station.'

Speck's eyes widened.

'No U-T! You can't. Please. You have to let me do this.'

U-T looked as confused as Speck felt. The bot darted looks from Nuis to Speck, and back to the Imperator's spaceship.

'Please,' Speck pleaded.

'B-but . . .'

Something gave in U-T's programming. With a little sigh, the little bot's grip loosened on Speck's arm. His ocular gaze fell to the floor.

'Best of luck, little brother,' the droid said in a voice that could hardly have been smaller. 'Please come back to us.'

Speck swallowed. He loved his brother more than he could ever comprehend. Rushing forward he gave U-T a hug, embracing his cold metal chassis, pointy corners and all.

'I will,' Speck promised and, with a final glance, he turned and darted the final fifty metres to the Imperators' ship.

It was only as he started to run that he realised he might have left it too late. The ship's ramps were already receding. Somewhere behind him he heard Nuis bleeping in fevered panic.

I'm not going to make it, he thought as a wave of anxiety washed over him. Then the hangar doors will open and I'll be sucked out into space. What will mother-bot think then? The thought was too terrible to even consider, and so, with a final burst of energy, he leapt through the air, landing on the craft's receding ramp. Scrabbling to his feet he found the port door directly before him – but it was nearly closed! With a gasp, Speck dove for the gap at the bottom, sliding beneath the thick metal and into the ship's interior just as the door slammed shut behind him.

Speck lay face down on the floor, enveloped in the dark and breathing heavily. The sound of the alarm was cut. The soft hum of the ship's engines and his own panting breath were all he could hear.

No. Not all he could hear. There was another noise too. A familiar sort of a noise. A buzzing hum.

Speck's eyes widened. It couldn't be.

He rolled over to find a glowing red eye hovering just above him.

'Nuis! What are you doing? You should have stayed with U-T.'

The little drone snapped back at him with a series of blips and bleeps, to which Speck sighed. 'I suppose you have your responsibilities too, hey?'

Nuis bleeped affirmatively, eye glowing green.

Speck couldn't help but smile. 'Well, I guess it's just you and me now.'

He looked around but was hardly able to see a thing in the darkness that swamped the inside of the Imperators' ship.

'How do they see in here?' he wondered to Nuis. 'Maybe it is a good thing you came along. At least now you're here I can maybe see where I'm going.'

Nuis bleeped happily and increased the brightness of its glowing eye, illuminating the shadows. Before them stretched a long corridor.

'Come on,' Speck whispered. 'Let's go find somewhere to hide.'

Speck felt the engines roaring somewhere far below as the pair began to make their way down the corridor. He got the sensation that the ship was moving, drifting through the hangar doors and out into open space.

'I've never been on a spaceship that wasn't the Library before,' Speck said to Nuis as they went. 'It feels strange.'

Nuis bleeped in acknowledgment. The sensation

was very strange indeed. Speck had to put a hand against the wall of the corridor just to stop himself from toppling over as the ship continued drifting out into space. It seemed like there was so much he didn't know about the Galaxy. He'd hardly left the Library's hangar and already he was far out of his depth.

He took another deep breath and felt stability return to his legs. Nuis was still by his side, bleeping quietly with concern.

'It's okay, Nuis,' he said. 'We'll be all right.'

Nuis blooped in agreement and began to float ahead, guiding Speck's way through the ship's interior. The corridor continued winding and it wasn't long before they arrived at an intersection. There were three separate corridors to take. They all looked identical.

'Which way do you think we should go?' Speck asked. The little drone flashed its light down each of the three corridors, one at a time, before returning to Speck's shoulder and giving a quizzical bleep.

'I suppose we should just choose one,' Speck said. 'Let's try left.'

Nuis bleeped its approval.

'I suppose it doesn't matter as long as we don't bump into any of the – oof!'

Speck grunted. He had just been turning the corner when he collided with something large and solid. He looked up with surprise to find a hulking

Imperator staring straight down at him. Its small, squinting eyes blinked in surprise and its large snout quivered as it sniffed the air.

'Stowaway!' the Imperator roared, one of its four arms pointing accusingly at Speck's stunned form. 'No stowaway allowed!'

The Imperator raised its laser rifle, pointing it directly at Speck. Speck froze. There was nowhere to run. He was speechless. How could his adventure come to an end so soon?

But then a blue light enveloped the imposing soldier. The creature's squinty eyes widened with surprise as it began to float away from the ground, dropping its firearm in surprise. Speck looked up to see Nuis emitting an anti-grav net from its blinking eye. It bleeped erratically as it focused the anti-grav's beam. He knew what it was trying to tell him: 'Run!'

Speck broke from his frozen stupor and hurtled past the Imperator, speeding blindly down the corridor.

'Stowaway!' came the Imperator's bellow from behind him. The soldier's loud voice thundered down the corridor. Speck knew it would be a miracle if none of its fellows heard it.

He was in trouble. Big trouble.

He came to an intersection and rounded a corner, and then another corner and then another corner. He was more lost than ever, and there seemed to be no end to the twisting labyrinth of corridors.

A sharp noise echoed from behind him and Speck swung around to find another of the hulking aliens towering over him, dull eyes watering as it examined his small, unimposing frame.

'Found stowaway!' it said, raising the rifle in its arms with a crooked grin on its face.

Speck took a deep breath and prepared for the worst. He closed his eyes and felt his heart hammering in his chest.

But, before the laser rifle could fire, something cold and hard cracked Speck over the back of the head with a disorientating wallop. Before Speck knew what was happening, he was hitting the metallic floor, his whole body stinging and his mind sinking into darkness. He had no idea if the laser rifle had even fired, for his ears heard only silence as his vision faded to black.

6

The Gumu Warren

When he woke up, Speck felt a hand gripped round his ankle. It was dragging him along the floor of a small duct, even more cramped than those found aboard the Library. Whatever had hold of him gave off one of the worst smells Speck had ever encountered in his life and was muttering to itself in an alien language of nervous gabbles and squeaks. He tried to crane his head to get a better view, but the smell only grew worse and his aching skull sparked furiously in protest. Instead, he let out a soft groan and his captor's mumbling ceased instantly.

'Ah. You wakey now, yes?' the creature asked in common speak. 'You lucky I find you in time. Big hulker about to make you go splat.'

The creature didn't sound too menacing. Its tone was affectionately grumpy, like mother-bot when she'd been on low power mode all day.

'What happened?' croaked Speck.

'You been rescued,' said the mysterious being who

he couldn't quite see. 'I heard them hulker all do big bellow. Stowaway here! Stowaway here! So loud. Hurt Yabba's ears. Me save you from rude hulker.'

'Oh,' said Speck, realising that the creature must have been referring to the Imperator when it said 'hulker'. 'And who are you exactly?'

'Me?' said the creature, sounding a little taken aback. 'You not heard of famous Yabba before?'

Speck shook his head. 'I'm sorry, but I haven't. Is Yabba the name of your species?'

'Yabba is name of me!' said the little creature feistily. 'Yabba of the Gumu tribe. Very famous Gutterling is Yabba.'

So it was one of the Gutterlings who had rescued him! That's why they were in one of the ship's many service ducts. The Gutterlings must use a similar system to the Library's utility bots in order to get around the Imperators' ship.

At that moment, the duct widened ever so slightly and the Gutterling released Speck's ankle. Speck could finally sit up and see the creature who had saved him.

Yabba, for his part, looked very proud of himself. He was only half Speck's height and covered head to toe in coarse fur. Wilting, bat-like ears protruded from the side of his head, and large beady eyes were set deeply into his face. He wore a dull grey tunic that exposed his furry chest and Speck could see a mysterious white symbol that looked like a lopsided

'T' dyed into the greasy fur there.

'Thank you for saving me,' said Speck, slowly growing accustomed to the little creature's stench. 'I don't know what I would've done if you hadn't been there.'

'You go splat,' replied the Gutterling. 'Yabba tell you that already.'

Speck frowned. The part about going splat he did understand, but there was one part of the rescue he was still confused by.

'Hang on. If the Imperator didn't get me then what was it that hit me on the head?'

'Ah,' and suddenly the rat-like creature was shuffling his feet bashfully. 'Yabba maybe make tiny mistake. Maybe come out of service hatch with little too much gusto. Hatch maybe hit human on head. Big wallop!'

'You're telling me,' Speck muttered, putting a hand to the tender egg-size lump that had formed on the back of his head.

'Ah, yes. Yabba sorry about this, but better than laser gun, no? You very lucky, now guest on Gutterling ship.'

'Gutterling ship?' Speck pondered aloud. 'I thought this ship belonged to the Imperators?'

'Ha!' Yabba scoffed. 'That what they all think. But who build ship? Gutterling do. Who make ship go? Gutterling do! Imperator are lucky to be passenger on mighty Gutterling craft!'

Speck muttered an apology and Yabba shrugged his scrawny shoulders, the insult already forgotten.

'So what does Yabba call human?'

Speck frowned again for a second, before realising that the Gutterling was trying to ask him for his name. He told the filthy little creature and Yabba nodded with an air of sage wisdom.

'Speck. This good name. You feel well enough to crawl, human Speck? Yabba tired of dragging heavy human and we must be going fast.'

'Yes, I think I can crawl,' Speck replied.

'Good. Now come along quickly. I take you to Gumu warren, home of Yabba's tribe.'

And with that, the Gutterling scuttled away down the duct. Speck twisted onto his belly and hurried to follow.

It felt like he crawled for an age, his elbows and knees crying out in pain from the cold metal, with only the incomprehensible mutterings of his rescuer to guide him, along with the occasional: 'Hurry human Speck,' or 'You mind gap here.' Eventually, just when Speck thought he might not be able to go any further, the dim light brightened and Speck realised they must be nearing their destination. He noticed more ducts joining the one he was crawling down – like many small streams flowing into a river – and from these openings he spied the wide eyes of more Gutterlings staring out at him.

'You be a mighty strange sight for many here,

human Speck,' chuckled Yabba. 'Lots of Gutterlings never see human before, especially inside warren. You lucky. Not many non-Gutterling see such wondrous place.'

Or smell such a place, thought Speck, as he held his hand to his nose. But despite the stink Speck found himself enraptured by the filthy little creatures, whose numbers only increased the deeper into the warren he went.

'Yabba, what does that "T" mark on all their chests mean?'

'Oh, that is mark of Gumu tribe,' Yabba smiled proudly. 'All Gutterling dye fur with symbol to show they are proud to be part of most best Gutterling tribe in Galaxy.'

'That sounds nice,' said Speck, wondering what it would be like to be part of a tribe. The utility bots on the Library looked after each other, sure enough, but everything they did was for the Keepers and, other than M-T and U-T, they hardly understood the concept of friendship. The Gutterlings, on the other hand, were the stark opposite. As Yabba waddled through the warren his fellow tribe members waved and greeted him merrily in their peculiar language.

'Do you know everyone in the warren?' Speck asked Yabba and the Gutterling chortled at the question.

'More like everyone know Yabba,' said the Gutterling. 'Yabba very famous. Yabba is most well-respected scientist of entire Gutterling race!'

'I see.' Speck eyed the little creature's dirty rags.

'Human Speck seem surprised,' said the Gutterling, casting an eye back at his guest.

'Not at all!' Speck protested, hoping he hadn't offended his new friend. 'Just – where I come from – droids look after the ship and that's it. We're not allowed to be anything other than cleaners or engineers. I thought Gutterlings were the same.'

'Well, all Gutterling *are* engineer,' said Yabba, scratching his beard fluff with a yellowed claw. 'But that not all Gutterling do. If all Gutterling do only one thing it be very boring, don't you think?'

'I suppose so,' said Speck.

'Yabba decide he want to be scientist when he young Gutterling. That why Yabba learn to speak many language and that why Speck lucky Yabba find him. Not many Gutterling speak common tongue.'

'Oh,' said Speck. He supposed he had been very lucky after all.

'Righto. Here we are,' announced Yabba suddenly, coming to an abrupt halt. 'Hurry now.'

Suddenly Speck felt Yabba's tiny hands shoving him sharply in the ribs and he was falling into one of the many side tunnels. The tunnel immediately sloped down and before Speck knew what was happening, he was sliding, unable to stop himself.

'Yabba!' he cried out in alarm, but the Gutterling was already gone from view as he plummeted down the chute at break-neck speed.

Dank air rose up to meet him as he slid faster and faster – and then he was piling out onto level ground, tumbling over and over.

Speck clenched his eyes shut, fearful of what he might find before him should they be open. But when he did finally look up, he was shocked to find himself in the most charming little living room he had ever seen. Small lamps cast warm light across cosy furniture made from repurposed junk and draped in colourful knitted throws. A little fireplace sat in the corner of the room, upon which sat a bubbling pot of stew, and the whole room was coated floor-to-ceiling in soft, spongy furs.

A moment later Yabba came shooting out from the bottom of the chute, rolling out onto the soft carpet with a whoop of excitement. With a hearty laugh the greasy being scrambled to his feet, patting down his fur and calling out in the chirpy Gutterling language.

At his chirps, three wide-eyed Gutterlings peered out from behind the couch where they'd evidently been hiding. One was an adult. The other two still young. The adult chirruped animatedly and Yabba replied with wheezing laughter.

'Yabba family hide from stranger,' Yabba explained to a perplexed Speck. 'Wife Podo think stars falling down when big human come crashing down warren chute!'

'Oh, I'm sorry,' Speck said, casting an embarrassed glance at Podo, but Yabba merely batted the apology away.

'Nonsense, friend Speck. Important thing is we made it just in time.'

'Just in time for what?' asked Speck, and as if in answer a deep rumbling echoed up from somewhere far below. A cry went up from Yabba and his family and Podo quickly busied herself fastening a lid to the simmering pot of stew.

'Hold on, human Speck,' urged Yabba as the creature gripped onto an exposed pipe. 'We be doing light-jump.'

'Light-jump?' Speck asked, but he hardly had time to comprehend. Just as he grabbed hold of the same pipe, he was hit by the most bizarre sensation he had ever felt in his entire life. It was like when he had fallen from the vent in the hangar of the Grand Orbital Library, but instead of falling, he was being flung in all directions at once. For a moment Speck was lifted fully from the ground, and if he hadn't been holding the piping he would have been tossed across the room. Now he could see why the living room was coated in soft furs! The whole sensation was entirely unbearable and yet Yabba and his family yelled out in excitement the entire time.

The feeling stopped as suddenly as it started, and the Gutterlings' cheers died down with several satisfied sighs of contentment. Speck's stomach was still heaving. He inhaled deeply, trying not to throw up, and saw Yabba grinning at him.

'You no like light-jump?' asked the creature, bemused. 'Maybe it not so fun for human, but it quite the thrill for Gutterling.'

'What just happened?' Speck asked.

'We jump to light-speed,' said Yabba casually. 'Spaceship now travelling very fast.'

'Really?' Speck raised an eyebrow. 'I've never travelled at light-speed before.'

'Yabba can tell,' chuckled the little Gutterling. 'Your face go very white.'

Speck laughed bashfully. He couldn't believe he was actually travelling at light-speed. Of course, he knew that if you wanted to get anywhere in the Galaxy you had to travel very fast indeed – the Galaxy was extremely large after all – but still, the idea that he was now going as fast as light boggled his mind.

For a moment a wave of sadness washed over him, as he realised that he was travelling further and further away from the only place he'd ever called home. There would already be an unimaginable distance between him and his family. Podo chirruped softly and Speck looked up to see that she was watching his sombre face.

'Yes, human Speck does look very sad,' Yabba said, agreeing with his wife. 'Tell us what troubles you, friend Speck, while we prepare meal.'

Speck sighed and told his story to the Gutterlings as they served up a surprisingly tasty dish of thick stew. He told them all about the Night Eaters and the trick the Starchild played on him, and as he recounted his tale, Yabba translated Speck's words to his family, who listened in attentive silence.

The silence continued for a moment after he concluded his tale – the only sound being the scraping of cutlery against the bottom of near empty bowls – and the two youngest Gutterlings soon clambered over to Speck and embraced his legs tightly. He was wholly unsure whether the tears in his eyes were due to the heartfelt gesture or the dire stench that emitted from the juvenile creatures.

'This mighty sad tale, human Speck,' Yabba concluded. 'But may I ask, what make you think you can catch such dangerous creature when you can't even stand up to one single hulker?'

Speck looked at his feet, doubt filling his mind. Yabba was right. He was a fool for even thinking he could help bring the Starchild back. He should have just stayed on board the Library and let the adults take care of things.

'I don't know,' he said quietly. 'But I have to try.'

Podo began squeaking enthusiastically and as Yabba listened he nodded thoughtfully.

'Wife Podo think that Speck has brave heart of Gutterling, and Yabba agrees. We wish to proclaim human Speck a friend to Gumu tribe and all

Gutterling race. Now, how can Gumu tribe help friend Speck with his noble quest?'

Speck thought for a moment. He was so lost and uncertain. He didn't even know where to begin asking for help.

'Well,' he said, 'it would be great to know where it is that we're heading.'

'Why, that is easy,' said Yabba. He laughed heartily. 'We are on course to Calestine. It must be where this Starchild was tracked to.'

'Calestine?' Speck repeated dumbly. 'I've never read about that planet before.'

'Not planet,' Yabba corrected. 'Calestine is moon. Most dangerous moon there is. No laws. Very popular place for outlaws – and pirates.'

'Pirates?' echoed Speck, feeling his knees go weak. 'Like space pirates?'

'Very same,' Yabba said. 'Certainly no place for young defenceless human.'

Speck bit his lip.

'Well, there's no going back now,' he said with a resigned sigh. 'I suppose I'll have to try. I wonder why the Starchild is going to such a horrid place?'

Yabba shrugged. 'Who know? All Gumu tribe know is that Calestine is very dangerous place. Yabba would come with new friend, but Yabba must stay on ship. Otherwise, all engines come crashing to standstill.' Yabba scratched his chin for a moment, muttering in the Gutterling language as he mulled the problem over, when Podo suddenly emitted a series of sharp, excited chirrups.

Yabba's beady eyes widened. 'Of course! Silly Yabba! There is a Gutterling on Calestine called Shegga. Shegga have no tribe but will help out friend of Gumu for sure.'

'Really?' gasped Speck, finally feeling a little hope reigniting. 'Thank you!'

'It nothing,' said the Gutterling, waving away the thanks. 'Last that Yabba hear, Shegga work at a tavern in the settlement there. What it called? Eternal Eclipse Tavern. That the one. You just tell Shegga words of friendship and he help you find Starchild.'

'Words of friendship?' Speck asked.

'Yes,' said Yabba. 'You just say to Shegga: chimi choro yoko. Then he know you friend of Gutterling. You remember words? Chimi choro yoko.'

'Chimi choro yoko,' repeated Speck, trying to imprint the words into his brain. 'Thank you, Yabba. But how am I even going to get to the Eternal Eclipse Tavern if this moon is as dangerous as you say?'

'Ah!' Yabba cried suddenly, perking up. 'Sure, it dangerous if you look like small vulnerable human boy, yes, but it much less dangerous for big scary human. You wait here, friend Speck.'

And with that Yabba scurried further into the warren, coming back a moment later clutching a silver length of material in both hands.

'You put this on,' said the Gutterling proudly,

holding the material up to him. 'This Yabba's proudest achievement. Yabba only ever made three of them in entire life!'

Speck took the silver outfit and held it up before him. It looked like the wetsuit he was given when the water tank clogged on the Grand Orbital Library and he had to dive beneath the water to fix it. This was a job that was always given to Speck – robots weren't great with water.

He started to don the outfit, feeling foolish as he pulled it over his existing jumpsuit. When he was done, Yabba produced a small console from his satchel and attached it to a power conduit on the suit. He pressed a few buttons, and suddenly Yabba's family gave out an ecstatic shout.

Speck frowned. He felt no different. All he felt was very silly.

'Here,' said Yabba, handing Speck a pocket mirror. Flipping it open, Speck nearly cried out in alarm, for the reflection looking back at him wasn't his at all. It was the face of the most fearsome old space pirate he'd ever seen.

'How?' he gasped. He examined the wrinkly face of the old, grizzled man staring back at him.

Yabba chuckled to himself proudly.

'Yabba call it phantom suit. Creates hologram all around Speck's body. Make him look just like ugly old pirate.'

Speck grinned and watched in amazement as the

fearsome old man grinned back at him in the mirror. As well as the deep wrinkles etched into his new face, he sported an eyepatch, a bulbous boil on his nose, and a deep, angry-looking scar that ran across one cheek.

'Speck is a short pirate, but short pirate better than no pirate at all,' murmured Yabba. 'Speck just make sure he careful what he touch. It only hologram mind you!'

Speck moved his hand up to his head and watched as his fingers went straight through the face of the pirate. He would have to remember not to scratch his nose while he was on Calestine, no matter how much it itched.

'It's wonderful, Yabba,' said Speck, hardly able to contain his excitement. 'You really are the most brilliant scientist there is!'

'Yabba knows,' the Gutterling said proudly. 'Yabba told you that already.'

Speck smiled and looked back at his new reflection. He promptly let his face fall into a variety of different angry expressions. No one would go anywhere near him looking like this! Maybe he would stand a chance after all.

'Now, it be a few hours until we reach Calestine,' said Yabba. 'Me think we could all do with a little rest before we arriving.'

Speck could hardly agree more. The Gutterlings made up the couch with comfy furs for him to sleep on and he'd hardly lain down before he drifted into a deep, content sleep. Maybe everything would work out fine. He dreamt of using his new phantom suit to catch the Starchild and bring it back to the Library, and in his dream even Giddius Monk was bowing before him and calling him a hero.

7

The Stranded Pirates

The landing jets roared as the Imperator's colossal ship approached the surface of the moon, Calestine. Speck stumbled and nearly fell. He was struggling to keep up with Yabba as the Gutterling led him along one of the spaceship's many winding service corridors.

'Hurry, Speck!' urged the little scientist. 'Big hulker Imperators will be roaming corridors very soon. We go to Gutterling's service hatch. Then you sneak out while Imperators not looking! Brilliant idea if Yabba does say so himself.'

Speck nodded, and as he did so he caught his reflection in the mirrored metal surface of the corridor. Though it wasn't really his reflection. He hadn't quite got used to the gnarled old face of the space pirate that stared back at him.

Speck had left Yabba's home shortly after the horrific jump back out of light-speed. He'd only just managed to keep his lunch down before Yabba was excitedly scampering off, yelling for him to follow. He had given a hasty hug to Podo as well as Yabba's children before being whisked away.

'Chimi choro yoko. Chimi choro yoko,' he panted under his breath, as he was led down the many sprawling corridors of the Imperators' ship. It was the phrase of friendship he had to remember. All he had to do was find Shegga and tell the Gutterling those words. Then everything would be okay.

Speck was so caught up in his own thoughts that he practically bowled into Yabba as the Gutterling finally came to a halt. They had reached the service hatch: a small, round porthole. As Speck looked through, he saw the sprawling expanse of an arid landscape. Deep craters and glittering aquamarine rocks were the only features to break up the sand stretching out toward the horizon.

Below the descending ship was a dark canyon, carved into Calestine's surface. Within this deep crevice Speck could make out what appeared to be a sprawling shanty town, with makeshift buildings hanging from the valley's steep sides. Even from the distance they were at, Speck could make out spaceships of all shapes and sizes sitting on the shifting sands.

'Smuggler's Gulch,' murmured Yabba. 'It mighty fearsome place. You be awful careful, friend Speck.'

'I will,' said Speck as bravely as he could. Yabba offered him a lopsided smile.

'You be doing good to deepen your voice too,' the Gutterling said. 'Yabba run out of voice disguisers. Gave his last one away years ago.'

Speck nodded. 'I hadn't even thought about that. How about this?' He cleared his throat and let a deep voice growl up from the depths of his lungs. 'Is this better, ye – salty, star . . . dog?'

Yabba looked at him skeptically. 'You maybe better keeping mouth shut and finding Shegga as soon as possible.'

Speck's cheeks flushed, but before he could say another word, the spaceship hit the moon's surface with a heavy thud. The whole fabric of the ship seemed to reverberate angrily before the hum of the engines died down and the whirlwind of dust slowly settled.

Speck let out a deep breath.

'Thank you, Yabba,' he said. 'For everything.'

The little Gutterling looked at him warmly. 'It be my pleasure. Friends help friends. Now go, or else it will be too late.'

The furry creature tapped on a console and the service hatch opened. As it did, a warm gust of dry air blasted Speck in the face, along with a smattering of scratching sand.

Before he could lose his nerve, Speck crept down the service ramp and onto the sand, quickly making for a nearby shack. Hiding around the corner of the abandoned building, he watched as the Imperators disembarked from the ship in ordered squads, laser rifles held in itching hands.

Speck was about to follow the soldiers into town when a familiar noise rose on the wind. He paused. He knew that sound. Scanning the immediate area, he let out a cry of surprise when he saw a little security drone bobbing aimlessly above the sand.

'Nuis!' Speck called in a sharp whisper. 'You're all right!' The drone peered up and spotted Speck. Its eye immediately glowed red as it neared him cautiously.

'Nuis? What's wrong? It's me,' Speck said. And then he realised why the drone was afraid. It couldn't recognise Speck. He was in disguise.

'Oh,' he said, as understanding dawned. 'I'm not really a scary pirate. It's just a hologram.'

He moved a hand to his head and waved his fingers through the hologram so the drone could see his real face hiding beneath. The security drone's eye immediately turned green and Nuis bleeped happily as it bobbed in the air.

'I'm glad the Imperators didn't splat you,' Speck said as the bot bleeped merrily by his side. 'Thank you for saving me, Nuis.'

Nuis bleeped nonchalantly, as if to say it was no big deal. Speck quickly explained the new plan to the little bot – that he had to locate the Eternal Eclipse Tavern and Shegga. Nuis listened quietly and nodded affirmatively as Speck concluded his retelling and, after he was done, they made their way into the shanty town.

Immediately they were swallowed by a thriving crowd. Smuggler's Gulch was bustling with activity. It took all of Speck's concentration just to avoid bumping into any of the hundreds of angry-looking inhabitants on the town's main drag. A market appeared to be in full swing, where creatures of all shapes and sizes were calling out to passers-by, offering their many exotic wares. The din of a hundred different languages being shouted at once washed over Speck.

'It's so busy,' Speck whispered to Nuis. 'I never knew there were so many beings in the Galaxy.'

The drone bleeped in acknowledgment as it stared warily at the crowd. Suddenly a squadron of Imperators came charging through the crowd and beings cried out as they struggled to move out of the soldiers' way.

Speck's eyes widened and he quickly ducked behind the nearest market stall, only able to breathe a sigh of relief again once the Imperators had passed. He'd have to be more careful if he was ever going to find Shegga in the Eternal Eclipse Tavern, and he'd have to find the tavern soon.

But there were too many buildings to search in Smuggler's Gulch and the canyon stretched on for miles. Finding a single inn would be like finding a needle in a haystack.

'I think we need to ask for directions,' Speck whispered to Nuis.

He scanned the crowd and zoned in on a pitiful creature slumped behind a market stall. Its body was no more than a slime-covered blob with one dull eye peering out from the top of the mound. Speck glanced at Nuis and the pair made their way over cautiously.

'Um, excuse me – sir,' said Speck. The creature's eye didn't move. It merely stared out into the crowd.

'I don't suppose you know where to find the Eternal Eclipse Tavern?'

The blob being didn't even move, and Speck looked up to Nuis with a shrug as if to say, 'I tried.' However, the drone continued to stare at the sad little creature intently.

'This is hopeless, Nuis,' Speck sighed. 'Let's find a being who can –'

But he was stopped short, as suddenly the creature's eye flicked up to him and, from beneath the layers of slime, a thick trunk emerged, also coated in a goopy layer of mucus. Speck watched in alarm as the creature pointed with its trunk and began emitting deep, guttural noises.

Speck sighed again. This really was no help. He didn't understand slime-talk. But then, out of the corner of his eye, he realised that Nuis was still focused on the creature, almost as if it were listening . . .

'Do you understand what it's saying, Nuis?' Speck asked, amazed.

The creature finished making its noises and Nuis looked up to him and bleeped happily. Its eye glowed green and it zoomed off down the main drag. Speck grinned. He couldn't believe it.

'Thank you, sir!' he said to the slime-being in a very un-pirate-like manner, bowing deeply as he chased after Nuis through the dusty crowd.

Speck pursued the little security drone down a labyrinth of back alleys and side streets and it wasn't long before he was standing in front of a shabby stone building carved straight into the rock wall of the valley. A sign hung above two large doors, scrawled in a language Speck couldn't read, but beneath the words was adorned the image of a darkly silhouetted moon. An eclipse!

'The Eternal Eclipse,' Speck whispered. Within the dusty windows, the interior was ominously dark. The tavern didn't look like the most inviting place in the Galaxy. Nuis was looking at Speck, evidently thinking the exact same thing.

'Don't look at me like that,' Speck said. 'It's the best plan we've got.'

As soon as he entered the tavern, Speck felt more out of place than he'd ever felt in his life. The inn was deathly quiet, and it looked like a tornado had recently blown through. Broken tables and shattered stools lay scattered everywhere, cobwebs hung from the ceiling and the dust that had blown in from outside remained unswept on the stained ground. A smattering of dark figures occupied several rotting booths, seemingly trying to stay away from the flickering light of the single lantern.

Speck held his nerve. Picking a seat at the bar, he found himself sitting next to a group of three ruffians. Trying desperately to avoid any eye contact with the dark trio, he searched for a sign of his Gutterling contact, but the bar was deserted. He was just about to turn and head back out again when a Gutterling, filthy and unkempt even by their filthy standards, padded out from behind the bar. A dark, crimson tattoo was branded across the Gutterling's face, and its pierced ears drooped low, burdened with a variety of metal rings.

Shegga! It had to be.

'Um, excuse me,' Speck said in his deepest voice. The Gutterling looked up, taking in his appearance with a shrewd eye.

'Yeah? What want?' snapped the Gutterling. 'You want grog?'

'Oh, no,' said Speck quickly. 'I'm not after a drink. I was just wondering, you wouldn't happen to be Shegga, would you? Shegga of the No-tribe?'

The Gutterling arched an eyebrow and looked about the bar. 'Maybe I is Shegga. What it to you?'

'You *are* Shegga?' Speck could hardly keep the excitement from his voice. 'My name is Speck. I'm a friend of Yabba of the Gumu tribe. He told me to say something to you . . .'

Speck frowned. His mind had gone blank. What was it that Yabba had told him to say? He shook his head, as if trying to dislodge the memory. Meanwhile Shegga's look of suspicion deepened.

'This some sorta joke, bud?' the Gutterling snarled.

'No, no. I was meant to say,' Speck continued. 'Chiki chomo yomo?'

No. That wasn't right. Why couldn't he remember? Speck let out a small grunt of frustration.

'You no friend of Gutterlings,' spat Shegga as he turned away.

'No, wait!' Speck stammered. 'I didn't mean that. I meant choko chomi yoko?'

At Speck's spluttering, one of the ruffians at the bar glanced up from his fellows.

'Well, would you look at that?' said the ruffian, pointing at Nuis. 'That's a security drone, ain't it? You must be a wanted man.'

Speck looked up with a start to see that all three of the ruffians had ceased their conversation and were peering at him keenly.

'Sorry?' Speck stammered, glancing between the pirates and the retreating Shegga.

'That drone you got with ya,' said the same ruffian with a toothy grin. 'Someone's keeping an eye on you.'

'Or maybe he's got an eye on us, Randall?' said the second of the ruffians, glancing at Nuis with a cautious eye. 'Maybe he's a spy.'

'Aye,' murmured the one called Randall. 'That wouldn't be very nice now, would it? If we were being spied on while we're trying to have ourselves a relaxing little drink.'

'I'm not a spy, I promise,' Speck stuttered as Shegga disappeared into the backroom. But there was no going after Shegga. The ruffian called Randall was already drawing closer. He was a human, with a slick, greasy-looking moustache and a long, arched nose.

As Randall drew closer, his dark eyes narrowed in deep suspicion. The sneer on his lips reminded Speck of Giddius Monk: snide and mocking. But then, just as quickly, the sneer gave way to a cheerful grin.

'I'm just grinding your gears, mate.' Randall laughed. 'There's no need to look so alarmed. The name's Dink. Randall Dink.' He extended a slender hand and offered it for Speck to shake.

Speck glanced down and hesitantly shook Randall Dink's hand, thankful that his gloves were the one part of his body that could be touched without breaking the hologram's illusion.

Randall pointed to his companions.

'These are my compatriots. The gal with the pallid complexion and the mean scowl is Vart, and our friend goes by the name Quilch.'

Speck greeted each in turn. Vart was a mean-looking being with near-translucent skin, icy blue lips, and dark eyes. She had limp grey hair which fell down from beneath a rotting bandana and she hardly moved when Speck introduced himself. The third ruffian was much smaller than the other two, and Speck recognised him as belonging to a race of beings known as the Quilkin. Speck knew very little about Quilkins, other than that they originated from a planet that was covered in thick forests. Quilch was dressed simply in a tattered robe, and his eyes twinkled as he chirruped at Speck in an alien language.

'Are you – space pirates?' Speck asked, half in awe and half in fear.

'Of course we are.' Randall grinned grimly. 'Half the scoundrels in this town are pirates, and the other half wish they were.'

The other two pirates weren't quite as taken by Speck as Randall was. Quilch twittered something darkly in its alien language and Vart nodded.

'True enough,' Vart said, in response to the Quilkin. 'He seems mighty ignorant about Smuggler's Gulch for an old-timer.'

Speck swallowed, worried he'd been found out already.

'I only just arrived today,' he said. 'I was a captive of the Imperators, but I managed to escape.'

It was only half a lie, Speck thought, and he was pleased to see that the pirates reacted as he had hoped they would.

'Escaping from the Imperators,' said Randall, with an impressed whistle. 'Now I'll drink to that.'

He raised his pitcher high before taking a long swig. Even the scowling Vart looked mildly impressed.

'To tell you the truth, I've never even met a pirate before,' said Speck cautiously.

Vart grunted. 'Well now you have. Not that you can really call us sorry lot pirates at this very moment. Can't do much plundering when we can't even set sail.'

'Don't you have a ship?' asked Speck.

'We have a ship,' Randall grumbled. 'But alas, we have no fuel for it. Rallium is what we need to hit light-speed, but we had to use the last of our supply to escape a fleet of Imperators. I'd say we hardly have enough now to escape the orbit of this damned moon, let alone cross the vast void of deep space.'

'Aye,' said Vart bitterly. ''Twas wondrous foresight from our fearless cappin' – as per usual.'

'That's our captain over there, the man in the corner,' added Randall.

Speck followed where Randall was pointing. There, sitting in a dimly-lit booth, was a human with dark skin, hunched over a flagon of ale and holding quiet conversation with a reptilian being.

'He's trying to trade the last of our loot for some measly drops of rallium,' muttered Randall in a low voice. 'The famous and mighty Captain Oran,' he scoffed mockingly.

Vart shook her head in disdain. 'He ain't that

mighty,' she said. 'The only reason they call him mighty is because he has that thing watching over him, day and night.'

Speck looked to the pale pirate questioningly.

'She's talking about the monstrosity standing next to the booth,' Randall said, in way of explanation.

Speck looked over and nearly gasped. He hadn't seen it before because it was standing so still, but there in the shadows next to the booth, was one of the most terrifying creatures Speck had ever seen. The lumbering giant seemed more robot than flesh. Its arms, legs and body were a hodgepodge of steel and skin and even from where he was sitting, Speck could see the wide variety of deadly weapons welded to its metal limbs.

'His name's Thrugg,' said Randall, lowering his voice. 'He's a gladiator from the planet Thrakkush. Somehow, he escaped them slave pits and now he's the personal guard of the captain. Believe me, if Thrugg sets his sights on you, you better wish you were already a goner.'

Speck gulped, thinking that maybe it might be best if he left and came back later. He could always try and get his message to Shegga when there were fewer gladiators from Thrakkush around.

'Thrugg's the only reason the captain is still in charge, in my opinion,' continued Randall, not noticing Speck's look of abject terror. 'Old Thrugg doesn't let anyone question the captain's command, or even touch a hair on the captain's precious head.'

As if in response to Randall's words, an angry hiss suddenly erupted from the corner booth. Speck glanced over to see the reptilian being reaching across the table for the captain. There was a glint of reflected light coming from the green creature's scaly hands. It was holding a knife!

But before the reptilian being could even get close to cutting the captain's throat, Thrugg took action. In one fell swoop the giant brought an abyssal hand crashing down on the reptilian creature's arm. The green creature hissed in agony, a wailing sound that split through the air.

'You no touch the captain,' rumbled the gladiator as it slowly lifted its hammer-like hand, releasing the pressure. The reptilian merchant immediately turned and fled the tavern, cradling the remnants of its shattered arm and hissing mournfully.

Captain Oran looked round at the rest of the tavern's patrons, all of whom were staring at the scene.

'Don't worry,' the captain said with an easy smile. 'He'll grow it back in a week.'

Randall turned from the scene and raised an eyebrow at Speck. 'And that's why you don't mess with the captain.'

Captain Oran got to his feet, eyeing the door through which the rallium merchant had just fled. He shook his head before making his way casually across to his fellow pirates.

'No luck with fuel then, Captain?' Randall asked innocently as Oran approached.

'Not yet,' Oran said. 'Negotiations became . . . strained.'

Randall shrugged. 'Well then, why don't you come for a drink with us and meet our new friend? Heck,' he said abruptly, shaking his head. 'I just realised, old-timer, I don't even know your name.'

'My – my name? It's, er, Speck,' he said quickly.

'Speck?' the captain murmured. 'Strange name for an old star-dog.' Over his shoulder, Thrugg murmured in agreement.

'Well, he is a strange one indeed,' chuckled Randall. 'Says he's never even met a space pirate before – in the middle of Smuggler's Gulch and everything!'

Speck tried to laugh along with the pirates, but there was something about the way Captain Oran was looking at him that he didn't like. He felt sweat begin to cling to his forehead.

'You don't sound much like an old star-dog either,' murmured Oran thoughtfully.

Speck felt his nerves getting the better of him under the captain's keen gaze.

He began to stumble backwards, away from the pirates, but no sooner had he moved than he felt his arm brush against an empty flagon of ale sitting on the bar. Immediately the captain's eyes fell to where the hologram ebbed away as it passed through the flagon.

'Ah,' said Oran with a wide grin. He looked round at his crew. 'Looks like you've all been hoodwinked.'

The pirates looked to their captain, confused.

'What do you mean, Cappin'?' Vart said.

Instead of replying, Captain Oran looked up to his towering bodyguard.

'Grab 'im, Thrugg.'

Before Speck even had a chance to run, one of the gladiator's huge metal hands had come down on his arm and he froze with fear as his phantom suit was punctured. He could only watch as the blue-glowing energy dissipated and the hologram dissolved away. He was just a boy again. Speck the lost, frightened little kid.

Vart got to her feet, her pallid face had turned a vivid shade of red.

'Hey! What is this?' she roared. 'He's just a kid!'

Randall was smiling thinly as if the facade merely amused him and Quilch was clucking angrily.

'A phantom suit,' murmured Oran approvingly. 'I've only ever seen one before in my entire life. Quite extraordinary.'

'Extraordinary?' Vart roared, her skin still the colour of blood. 'He made a fool of us!'

'He did,' Oran said thoughtfully, and Speck couldn't help but notice that the pirates were all reaching for their weapons. He also couldn't help but notice that Thrugg's grip was tightening and the gladiator's usually glassy eyes were beginning to focus squarely on him.

'Mighty rare and expensive those phantom suits,' the captain said to Speck with a pleasant smile. 'And as you can see, we're a little strapped for cash.'

Suddenly the captain had a blaster in his hand and it was pointed directly at Speck's face. 'So either you give it to us freely,' said Oran coolly, 'or we'll take it from you by force.'

8

Cry of the Starchild

Not too far away from the Eternal Eclipse Tavern, a scientist was darting across the interior of a dusty, ramshackle laboratory. He muttered to himself feverishly as he packed a bag, selecting items haphazardly from amongst his equipment. The being had orange skin, beady eyes and not a single hair on his bulbous head. Adjusting his glasses, he jammed a few test tubes into a case and zipped it closed.

The scientist patted his case for good luck – a habit of his – and was just making for the exit when a voice spoke out from the darkness.

'Where do you think you're going?'

The scientist froze. He glanced around the empty laboratory with wide eyes. The voice was soft like the wind and he found that he couldn't place the direction from which it came.

'Who's there?' the scientist called with a shaky

voice. There was no answer, and he quickly wished he'd thought to light a few more lamps. He scanned the room slowly, the sound of his own breath loud in his ears.

Then, with a ghastly *phwoomf*, a pair of blazing eyes ignited within the shadows of the room.

'I asked you a question,' said the voice from behind the blazing eyes.

'I'm going nowhere,' stammered the frightened scientist as he backed up against a tower of dusty microscopes.

The two blazing eyes narrowed with suspicion as they drew closer and from the shadows emerged the figure of the Starchild. Its feet twitched as they floated above the ground and it cocked its head inquiringly, peering down upon the cowering scientist.

'It looks like you are running away,' said the Starchild calmly. 'You wouldn't be running away now, would you?'

The scientist shook his head and accidentally fumbled his bag. The case fell sharply to the floor with a pitiful smashing of glass.

'You know who I am,' stated the Starchild. It was not a question.

The scientist nodded dumbly.

'And you are the scientist, Bizzabin, are you not?'

'Yes,' admitted the scientist miserably.

'Then it is you who I have been searching for.' A smile slowly spread across the leathery face of the Starchild.

'M-me?' Bizzabin squeaked. 'Surely there must be a mistake.'

'I am never mistaken,' said the Starchild. 'Your name was whispered to me. I heard it echoed across the eternal void when I turned to the stars for the answer to my question.'

Bizzabin swallowed. 'What question?' he said, already regretting the words as they left his mouth.

The Starchild's smile widened. 'Those who gave me life,' it said. 'Where are they?'

Bizzabin shuddered, his face a mask of fear.

'I can't –' the scientist babbled.

'You will tell me now!' bellowed the Starchild, and its eyes burned brighter than ever. Heat poured from them and Bizzabin felt the skin on his face begin to smoulder.

'All right!' whimpered the scientist. 'I'll tell you. Just please, have mercy on me.'

The scientist began talking, letting loose a torrent of hurried chatter. The Starchild backed away slightly as it listened to every last fear-stricken syllable fall from Bizzabin's lips, and it continued to listen all the way to his tale's spluttered conclusion.

'And, you see, that's about it. I promise,' Bizzabin said.

The Starchild didn't speak and, after a few seconds, it turned its back on the scientist. Bizzabin watched fearfully as the creature hung its head low. He noticed its shoulders were heaving.

It's crying, Bizzabin realised, and his heart

suddenly filled with pity. Maybe it isn't so terrifying after all. Maybe it's scared.

Bizzabin was just reaching out a comforting hand to put on the being's shoulder when the Starchild moved with blistering speed.

And what Bizzabin saw then made his blood run cold, for he had been very wrong. The Starchild's eyes blazed with fury, and suddenly Bizzabin understood that the Starchild's shoulders hadn't been heaving with sobs at all. Its whole body was in fact shaking with uncontrollable rage. Its hands were clenched into tight balls and, as it turned its head to the ceiling, it let out the most hideous scream Bizzabin had ever heard in his life.

And with the scream came the explosion.

The pirates were closing in around Speck when the windows of the Eternal Eclipse Tavern shattered, the door blew off its hinges, and a wave of force knocked them all flat to the ground. Hideous screaming burnt through the air and slowly died on the wind.

'What in the meteor-shower was that?' cried Captain Oran, back on his feet in a matter of seconds. 'Thrugg, go check it out. Now.'

The hulking Thrugg immediately released Speck's arm and manoeuvred his bulk through the gap where the tavern's doors had been only moments before. As the gladiator left, Speck glanced fearfully at the rest of the pirates, but it appeared that they'd already forgotten him. Instead, they were all crowding round the blown-out windows. Speck could only think to join them as they peered through to see what had caused such an explosion.

Outside, Smuggler's Gulch was a riot of panic. Beings of every shape and size were fleeing in all directions. Dust was billowing everywhere, snatched off the ground and whipped into a whirlwind of blinding grit. Anything that wasn't bolted down was rattling with a calamitous din. Speck watched as a desperate fish merchant tried to keep his daily catch from being whipped away by the vicious winds. Elsewhere, a whole cart of exotic fruit was being dragged along the sand as if caught on a giant fishing line. As Speck watched, he realised that all the debris was moving in a pattern, gravitating toward a single point in the distance: a building. Or, more accurately, the shell of a building.

'I've never seen anything like it before in my life,' said Randall in awe.

'I don't like it,' muttered Oran. 'Where's Thrugg? I lost him.'

Speck was surveying the scene for the hulking metal monster when his eye was caught by a solitary figure standing amongst the chaos. The figure wore the crimson cloak of a Night Eater, and Speck could just make out the glimmer of two sapphires glinting in the figure's mask. It was Giddius!

The Guild leader was facing the epicentre of the chaos with folded arms, looking oddly serene with the panic that surrounded him. His cloak whipped wildly around his figure as it too sought to join the swirling sand and debris that was blowing towards the wrecked house in the distance.

'What do we do, Cappin'?' Vart asked. Her skin had returned from blood red to its usual pale hue.

'I don't know,' admitted Oran. 'I'm not even sure what we're up against here.'

'I think I know how to find out,' Speck said. His eyes were still locked on Giddius, and before any of the pirates could say anything he ducked through the ruined tavern door and out onto the street.

'Nuis!' he called as he dodged through the crowd. The drone was by his side in an instant. 'Can you work out how to get my phantom suit working again? I think I'll need it.' The security drone blooped affirmatively as it floated round to the console sitting on his chest. A little claw protruded from under the bot's glowing eye and, after a little prodding, the little drone emitted a cheerful bleep of victory.

'Good work.' Speck smiled as he saw the disguised face of the grizzled space pirate reflected back at him in a nearby window.

'Excuse me!' Speck called out to Giddius as he drew closer, being careful to use his disguised pirate voice. 'I don't suppose you could tell me what all this ruckus is about?'

Giddius turned. Speck could imagine the

displeased look lying just beyond the Guild leader's obsidian mask, disgust evident in being addressed by such a lowly space pirate.

'It's a Starchild,' Giddius replied curtly. 'Not that I'd expect that to mean anything to a man of your . . . calibre, but we're about to see a taste of its formidable power. Quite fortunate really. Hardly any beings can claim to have witnessed such an extraordinary display of raw energy.'

The Starchild! Speck let out a very un-pirate-like squeak and turned to the centre of the destructive storm. He could just make out a small, child-like figure floating amongst the obscuring whirlwind of sand, clenched fists raised to the sky.

'I'd run along if I were you, little star-dog,' mused Giddius. 'This moon is about to get very cosy indeed.'

'What do you mean?' Speck asked, forgetting for a second to disguise his voice. Fortunately, Giddius was too enamoured with the storm to notice.

'The Starchild is doing what it was born to do,' the Guild leader continued. 'It's releasing its energy. So much, in fact, that it will all come collapsing back in on itself. Simply put – it's creating a black hole.'

Speck gasped, stepping back. A black hole! If a black hole formed this close to Calestine then – well, Speck didn't want to think of the consequences – but all he knew was that Smuggler's Gulch would soon cease to exist. And not just Smuggler's Gulch, but the whole moon!

'Can't it be stopped?' Speck asked meekly, but

Giddius was already shaking his head.

'Only the Starchild can stop it now. The black hole is still weak but it's only a matter of time. So, I'd suggest you get off this moon before it's too late. Everybody else will.'

Speck's panic blossomed. He thought about deactivating his phantom suit and pleading with Giddius to take him away on board the *Pilgrim*, but just as quickly the thought fizzled away. He had been the one to free the Starchild after all. He could just imagine Giddius' fury if he was suddenly confronted by the boy who had released his research subject in the first place.

Instead, Speck turned and pushed his way blindly through the crowd. Nuis was right beside him and gave out an alarmed cry as a large lumbering being came hurtling out of the crowd, colliding with Speck at breakneck speed and sending the boy spiralling to the ground. The drone was hovering above Speck's face in an instant, concerned bleeps ringing in his ear.

'I'm fine,' said Speck with a groan, but the console on Speck's chest wasn't. It gave out a final whine as it spluttered and died, and he was back to being just Speck again.

Struggling to his feet, Speck was greeted by the sight of a squad of Imperators preparing a barrage of laser-fire at the Starchild. The squad sergeant stood to one side, holding up two of its arms as it bellowed in a hoarse tone.

'Ready. Aim. Fire!' The sergeant brought its heavy arms down, and the Imperators let loose with their weapons. No sooner had the lasers left the guns than they were whisked away by the storm, sucked into the small dot of darkness that had appeared above the destroyed building.

I can see it, Speck realised. That's the black hole right there, and no one can stop it. The Imperators seemed to have come to the same realisation, for the sergeant hastily called a retreat and Speck could only dive to one side as the whole squadron of soldiers barrelled past him.

'Evacuate!' the sergeant cried as the platoon stormed down the street and past where Captain Oran and the rest of the pirates had just arrived.

'Kid!' the captain yelled over the wind as he helped Speck to his feet. 'What did you find out?'

'It's creating a black hole,' Speck said, pointing to the distant figure of the Starchild. 'This whole moon is about to be destroyed!'

The captain shared glances with the other nervous pirates.

'Back to the ship. All of you,' he commanded. 'We should have just enough fuel to get off this rock.'

'And then what?' Randall asked sceptically. 'Are we to just float around space for eternity?'

'One thing at a time,' snapped Oran. 'Now go!'

The crew burst into action and Captain Oran looked down at the uncertain Speck.

'Come on,' he said grimly. 'You'd better come with us. Your drone can come too. But I still want that phantom suit when this is all over.'

Speck let out a sigh of relief and he and Nuis both fell in line with the pirates, joining them as they made their way through the back alleys of Smuggler's Gulch.

The pirate's ship was on the far side of town, and by the time they were nearing it the streets were all but empty. All around, spacecraft were taking to the skies as the last of the town's residents fled the moon's surface. For a moment, the stars were blotted out and Speck looked up to see the gargantuan Imperator ship rising slowly into Calestine's atmosphere.

At least Yabba and the rest of the Gumu tribe will be safe, he thought to himself.

'There it is!' came a relieved shout from ahead. Speck turned round sharply to see an unimpressive spaceship sitting beneath the awnings of a row of market stalls. It was very dirty, and much smaller than the Imperators' ship – or even the *Pilgrim* – but Speck supposed he couldn't afford to be picky. Not with the whole moon about to collapse around him.

As the band charged across the last stretch of dust, the ship's embarkment ramp lowered and the crew bundled within. Speck and Nuis came scrambling up the ramp last. Almost before they'd even made it inside, he heard the ramp receding behind him again and the ship's hatch slammed shut with a hiss.

'Welcome aboard the *Dawnchaser*,' Oran said, darting a look at Speck as he took a seat in the flight deck's largest chair. 'No time for a tour, I'm afraid. I'd also suggest holding on. It's going to be a bumpy ride.'

Speck did as Oran suggested, staring wide-eyed as the pirates buckled into their various seats. Vart sat in the pilot's chair and moments later the ship rose unsteadily into the air as she pressed and pulled the many controls and levers. The hungry engines whined in protest as the thrusters struggled.

'I'll be amazed if we have enough fuel to even get off the ground,' Randall muttered darkly from his seat as he pored over a number of star-charts laid out before him.

'Thank you, Randall,' the captain said. 'If you have anything else productive to add, then I'm all ears.'

'Dumb, dumb navigator,' rumbled the imposing Thrugg from where he was stood near the flight deck's rear.

Randall glared at the gladiator, but kept his mouth firmly shut.

'Here goes,' said Vart. 'Easy does it.' Outside the

port window, the world was obscured by dust and sand as the gravitational winds continued to blow up a sandstorm.

'I'm flying blind,' Vart yelled.

'Hold your course,' Randall barked. 'We'll be fine if we just hold this line.'

'Easier said than done,' Vart grunted, weaving the ship between two pieces of debris that came soaring out of nowhere. The black hole was getting so strong now it was even beginning to break the moon itself into pieces, sending large boulders careening towards its dark embrace.

A ginormous shape loomed directly ahead of the ship from within the maelstrom. Speck's eyes widened as he spotted it. 'Look out!' he cried.

'I see it,' muttered Oran as the shadow took shape. It burst through the sandstorm and Speck saw the largest boulder he could ever imagine hurtling straight towards them.

'No time to go around,' Oran said. 'Quilch. Blast it!'

Quilch twittered happily and took aim. There was a flash of light as a laser snaked out from the ship's artillery and hit the boulder. The rock exploded into a heavy shower of tiny stones. The ship bucked and rolled as a thousand small pebbles bounced off its hull.

'We'll be out of the moon's atmosphere in a matter of seconds,' said Randall, eyes glued to his computer console. The sandstorm was beginning to clear and Speck could see the twinkling stars beyond.

'Step on it!' Captain Oran yelled as a whoop went up from the pirate crew.

Vart leant forward on the accelerator lever.

But nothing happened.

In fact, the ship wasn't going faster at all. It was beginning to slow down.

'What's happening?' Oran asked, looking across at his pilot. 'I said accelerate.'

'I am accelerating,' said Vart, her skin beginning to turn a sickly green.

'The black hole's too strong,' Randall whispered, voice laden with despair.

The ship continued to slow down, despite the engines giving full throttle. The *Dawnchaser* bucked and strained as it stopped moving forward at all. And then, slowly – ever so slowly – the ship began to creep backwards, reversing towards the black hole.

The pirates shared panic-stricken glances.

'Keep gunning those engines!' Oran barked.

'I can keep us steady but we're using up the last of our fuel,' Vart said.

'What do we do?' Randall asked in a trembling voice, but Oran didn't have an answer. He was wordless.

The whole ship rattled as the black hole sought eagerly to claim its victims. Speck knew he should have been terrified but found that he was oddly calm.

In fact, he was hardly paying attention. There was something at the back of his mind, niggling away. An important piece of advice that he'd once heard aboard the Grand Orbital Library. It was something that the High Librarian had said to him.

'We mustn't fear it,' he mumbled to himself thoughtfully.

Captain Oran gave him a curious glance.

'What, kid?'

Speck blinked. All the pirates were looking at him. Nuis gave him an encouraging bleep, as if urging him to continue his train of thought.

'It's something the High Librarian said,' he explained. 'He told me that creatures called space wyrms can control black holes, and the only reason they can do so is because they have no fear of them.'

Vart frowned. 'How's that going to help us now?'

Speck closed his eyes, trying to shut out the din of the roaring engines and the worried pirates. He had wondered what the High Librarian had meant. How could you show a black hole that you didn't fear it? Well, there was only one way Speck could think of, but it sounded insane.

'Maybe we're accelerating the wrong way,' Speck suggested. 'Maybe we should go towards it.'

'Did he just say what I think he said?' Randall said.

Quilch twittered furiously.

'What do you mean?' Oran demanded.

'The bravest thing I can think of doing right now

is the opposite of running away,' said Speck. 'We need to dive into the black hole as fast as we possibly can.'

'Dive into it?' Randall repeated, accompanied by more of Quilch's fearful twitters. 'He's gone mad! Quite mad!'

'You can't be serious,' said Vart, but Oran was silent. The captain stared levelly at Speck, then up to the expressionless Thrugg and finally out of the window to the shining stars as they began to disappear behind the blanket of the sandstorm once more.

'Captain, you can't be serious!' Randall demanded.

From the pilot's seat Vart shrugged. 'For what it's worth, Cappin', I don't think we have many alternatives at this point.'

'Help might come!' Randall said.

'No,' said Oran. 'It won't.'

The captain looked at Speck and nodded.

'Let's try it,' he ordered.

'Captain, please! Be reasonable!' said Randall, but no one was listening.

'Here goes nothing,' said Vart. 'Good luck everyone.'

And with a deep breath she released the bucking controls. The ship spun round to face the storm's centre, and for a second the world hung suspended in motion. Speck could see the black hole in the distance, no more than a dot. The town of Smuggler's

Gulch was no more, and the moon wasn't far behind. Speck watched as the moon was ripped apart, slowly eaten by the Starchild's creation. It was beautifully terrifying.

And then Vart leant forward on the ship's controls, the thrusters kicked in and the *Dawnchaser* hurtled into the abyss.

9

Lost in the Mist

The *Dawnchaser* dove into the black hole and Speck's world fell into chaos. He quickly discovered that jumping into light-speed was nothing compared to the experience of being crammed into a black hole.

In the black hole, the laws of space and time made no sense. His whole world became a dizzying kaleidoscope that moved so fast he felt sick. Up was down, and down was up. It was unbearable. He was no longer even a person but a mess of tangled limbs, and just when he was on the very edge of existence, it all came snapping back like an elastic band, pulled to breaking point. Speck was flung back. He could feel his feet shooting back up towards his body. He could see his knees once more. He was crushed, stretched, and crushed once more, and then he was through the black hole.

He had made it to the other side.

Speck opened his eyes. He hadn't even realised he'd had them closed, but he must have been clenching them shut with all his might, for the muscles on his face ached. To his vast relief, he found himself still on the flight deck of the pirate ship. Everything on board was as it had been before they had entered the black hole, but Speck could tell from the pirates' expressions that they had just been through the same mind-numbing experience he had endured. With wide eyes, they stared at each other, daring one another to speak first.

'Would somebody please tell me what in the star shower just happened?' Randall croaked from the navigation desk.

'We're alive,' said Vart. She was still clutching onto the ship's controls. Her skin had turned a shade of deep blue.

Quilch twittered excitedly and Thrugg began laughing in a deep monotone guffaw.

'We made it!' Vart said. Her scowl had broken into a grin.

All the pirates began to cheer, whooping with joy. Even Nuis was bleeping ecstatically by Speck's side.

'You saved us, kid,' said Captain Oran as he turned to Speck.

Speck beamed from ear to ear. His plan had worked! He wasn't sure how or why, but by diving into the black hole they had survived it. He felt his cheeks flush red with pride as Captain Oran clapped him on the shoulder, and the pirates continued to chatter excitedly. Randall seemed to be the only one who wasn't ready to share in the joy.

'I don't wish to sour the mood,' he said dryly, pointing out of the viewport, 'but before we get too carried away, maybe we should work out exactly where it is we are.'

The pirates quietened, and Speck looked out the viewport window to see that the ship was surrounded by dense white fog, swirling past in thick sheets.

'Maybe we're still in the black hole?' Vart suggested, but just as she spoke, a large shape came looming out of the fog. It was a colossal tree, reaching up from the depths far below.

'I don't think so,' said Captain Oran as the *Dawnchaser* sped past more of the colossal trunks. 'Unless you find giant trees inside a black hole.'

'Then where are we?' asked Speck.

Suddenly Quilch began twittering frantically in his alien tongue and the pirates turned to the wildly gesturing Quilkin. As they listened, Speck saw each of their faces falling in disappointment.

'What's he saying?' Speck asked, realising he was the only one who couldn't understand the Quilkin's twittered language.

'He says that he was trying to warn us before we dived into the black hole,' translated Oran.

'Warn us of what?' asked Speck. His stomach already tying itself in knots as the Quilkin continued to chirrup, and the horror on the crew's faces magnified.

'Quilkin legends say that black holes are in fact tunnels through the very fabric of space.'

'Tunnels?' echoed Speck, feeling a lump form in his throat. The pride he had been feeling only a moment before was all but extinguished.

'Aye,' murmured Oran. 'Like shortcuts. And, according to these legends, if you were to go through one of these tunnels then you would be catapulted to the far side of the Universe.'

'What?' gasped Vart, her face turning even paler than usual. 'You mean we've teleported?'

'It would seem so,' sighed Oran.

'And now we could be anywhere in the Universe,' said Randall, eyeing Speck darkly.

'Universe very big,' murmured Thrugg.

'And need I remind you all,' said Randall. 'We are still out of fuel.'

The pirates fell into silence as the seriousness of their situation dawned on them. It didn't seem to matter that moments ago they had celebrated surviving a black hole. The joy of that moment had quickly been quashed and replaced with despair.

'What are we going to do?' Vart asked.

'I don't know,' Oran replied. 'But first of all, we need to reserve our fuel and work out where we are. Any clues on the scanners?'

The pirates all busied themselves at various consoles. Speck stood where he was, fidgeting and feeling like a spare part. He wished he could be of more help, but he simply didn't know anything about being a pirate. All he felt was miserable. Thrugg must have noticed, for the gladiator rested one of his large metal fingers comfortingly on Speck's shoulder.

'It okay, human,' murmured the gladiator with a soft smile. 'Not your fault.'

Nuis concurred, with a comforting bleep of his own, but Speck still felt wretched. How was he supposed to know that this would happen?

'Seems like there's land below us, beneath all this fog,' reported Vart as she tapped at the console next to her controls. 'Lots of water too. Some sort of swamp would be my guess.'

'The air is breathable,' the captain added. 'Strange that a black hole should spit us out directly onto the surface of a planet, but I suppose we shouldn't complain. Take her down, Vart.'

'Aye, Cappin'.' Vart began guiding the ship down through the mist.

'I don't believe this,' whined Randall. 'Lost on an alien planet in the middle of deep space with no fuel! Another brilliant piece of leadership from the wonderful Captain Oran.'

At the navigator's words, Thrugg sprang forward with a deep growl.

'You no bad-mouth Captain,' rumbled the mechanical monster threateningly.

Then Quilch joined in, twittering angrily at the pair of them, and it wasn't long before the pirates had all fallen into heated debate. Speck could only watch as they all shouted at each other angrily, everyone attempting to blame someone else for what had happened. But Speck knew who was really to blame.

With a sigh, he turned and padded out of the flight deck and into the ship's empty corridors, Nuis by his side. It wasn't long before he found an empty storage shelf in the depths of the ship. It reminded him a little of his bed back on board the Grand Orbital Library. Pulling off the phantom suit, he rolled it into a makeshift pillow and curled into a tight ball, trying to imagine that it was all a bad dream. Perhaps when he opened his eyes again, he would find himself back home. M-T would be waiting, chiding him for sleeping in longer than he should have, but he wouldn't care that he was in trouble. He would be home with those that loved him.

'How did we get so lost?' Speck whispered to Nuis. It seemed like he just kept getting further away from home. Worst of all, his plans to recapture the Starchild were shattered, and he had no idea how much more damage that evil creature would do.

He must have fallen asleep at some point, because Speck eventually became aware that the ship was no longer moving and the corridors were devoid of any raised voices. He sat up groggily in his bed and rubbed the sleep from his eyes. Nuis had connected itself to a power terminal on the far side of the corridor, recharging its battery, but when it saw Speck getting up, it disconnected immediately, bobbing sluggishly over to greet him.

'We must have landed.' Speck yawned. 'Or run out of fuel.'

The flight deck was empty, and after searching the entirety of the ship, Speck discovered the port hatch open and the embarkment ramp fully extended. As he stood at the open door, he was hit by the icy chill of the alien planet's atmosphere. He wrapped his thin arms round his body for warmth and stepped out, tendrils of fog reaching out greedily to grasp at him. He was surprised to find that the ground of the planet was covered in soft, springy moss.

The pirates had made a temporary camp for themselves outside of the ship. A portable heater sat in the midst of a ring of benches and a plastic sheet had been set up like a roof to shelter them from the light drizzle that was falling. Visibility beyond the marshy clearing was poor, but the distant silhouettes of trees and bushes must have contained some wildlife, since Speck could hear a vast variety of chirps and whistles echoing in the distance.

The pirates were muttering to each other in low voices, but when Speck stepped into the makeshift camp, they all stopped as one and turned to face him.

'Speck, there you are,' said Captain Oran, clearing his throat. 'I decided it was best to make camp for the evening. We'll make plans in the morning when it gets light. Come get some food. Keep your energy up.'

Speck took the bowl of bland gruel that was offered to him by Thrugg and he sat down with the pirates around the spluttering electric fire. The food looked hideous, but he soon found he was far hungrier than he ever thought possible. It had been a long time since he'd eaten, after all.

'I think we owe you an apology,' said the captain after a while as he watched Speck picking at his food.

Speck looked around at the pirates. They all seemed sheepish, except Randall who was as indignant as ever.

'We all got a bit excited about our current predicament and forgot that, without you, we'd all be a lot worse off right now.'

'Yeah, the captain's right,' agreed Vart. 'You saved us and we didn't thank you for it. That wasn't very professional. Even pirates oughta be professional.'

'We bad pirates,' said Thrugg mournfully.

'And to put it bluntly, we're impressed kid,' continued the captain. 'It was quick thinking to suggest diving into the black hole – and brave too. If we ever get out of this whole predicament you should think about joining us.'

'Joining you?' said Speck. 'You mean become a pirate?'

'Yeah, why not? We have openings,' said Vart, poking her gruel with a spoon. 'We need a new cook for instance – desperately. No offence, Thrugg.'

Thrugg shrugged and Speck couldn't help but smile.

'I never knew that's how you became a pirate,' said Speck thoughtfully.

'There's no one way to become a pirate, kid.' Oran laughed. 'None of us exactly chose the pirate life. We all have a different story that brought us here.'

'What's yours, kid?' Vart asked. 'What were you doing in Smuggler's Gulch?'

Speck sighed and began recounting his story to the pirates, telling them how he had been tricked into releasing the Starchild and his journey to bring it back again. He told them about the Keepers and Giddius Monk, of the Imperators and his encounter with the Gumu tribe. As he spoke the planet's star finally set, and soon the only light left was the orange glow of the electric fire. After Speck concluded his tale, it felt like the little camp could be the only pinprick of existence in the whole Universe.

'I suppose I should be angry that it was you who released that thing in the first place,' murmured Vart when Speck had finally finished. 'But this Starchild sounds like a bully, and we've all been victims of bullies before.'

The rest of the pirates nodded solemnly. Even Randall didn't look as furious as Speck might have expected.

'Do you think everyone got off the moon in time?' Speck asked. The question had been preying on his mind ever since they made their escape.

'Kid, if there's one thing the residents of a place like Smuggler's Gulch are good at, it's making a hasty exit,' said the captain with a comforting smile. 'I'd guess that we were the last ones off that rock by a long shot.'

Speck nodded. It made him feel a little better, but not by much.

Vart shuffled along the bench and extended a hand. 'I suppose if we're going to be a crew for the foreseeable future then we should introduce ourselves properly,' she said. 'These lugs call me Vart, but that's my last name. My first name is Nephora.'

Speck shook Nephora's hand, her translucent skin glistening in the glow of the electric fire.

'I've never seen anyone like you before,' Speck said, marvelling at her skin. 'Not even as a visitor to the Library.'

'I'm a Ureyan,' Nephora replied. 'But an adult Ureyan isn't meant to have skin like mine. It's meant to settle on one colour when we grow up. That's what tells you which tribe you belong to. Except something went wrong with me. My skin never settled on a colour and I just ended up staying like this – forever.'

'And that's how you became a pirate?' Speck asked.

Nephora shrugged. 'I didn't fit in with my own people, and so eventually I went out looking for my own tribe. That's how I met this sorry lot.'

'You don't seem that bad to me,' Speck offered quietly.

'Thanks kid,' smiled Oran. 'We've all got similar stories. Quilch used to be a slave in the great asteroid mines. That robe he wears hides the scars left by his master's whip.'

Quilch chirruped sadly in acknowledgement and pulled the robe tight round his small frame.

'Well, I – for one – was born into the plundering life,' announced Randall with a tone of unmistakable pride. 'I hail from a long line of pirates, thieves, and cutthroats. The Dinks are pure scoundrels, the lot of us.'

'Explains a lot,' Nephora murmured under her breath, and Speck couldn't help but grin.

'Thrugg's tale very sad,' added the great giant suddenly as he sat cross-legged on the ground. 'Thrugg's tale still not even find its end.'

'Why not, Thrugg?' Speck asked.

'Thrugg is searching for princess,' said the gladiator, and a sad, faraway look came across his glassy eyes.

'Thrugg's is a miserable tale,' admitted Oran, resting a comforting hand on his bodyguard's immense arm. 'Thrugg comes from the planet Thrakkush. Do you know of it, Speck?'

'Only what I've read in the Library,' Speck admitted. 'And that's not much.'

'Aye,' said Oran. 'Thrakkush is a foreboding planet near the outer rim of the Galaxy. It was once home to a mighty kingdom. But one day, not too long ago, the people of the planet decided they didn't need a king anymore, so they had an uprising. The royal family were overthrown, but the night before the royal palace was captured, the princess managed to escape. She didn't get far. Lost and alone in the streets of the capital city, she was captured and sold as a slave in the great fighting pits.'

'No good fighting pits,' rumbled Thrugg.

'The princess was forced to work,' continued the captain. 'Cleaning the cells of the gladiators who fought there. That's where she met Thrugg. You see, the people of Thrakkush enjoy nothing more than watching innocent creatures fight for their own amusement, and they even decided to construct their own gladiators – the perfect fighting machines – to satiate their thirst for blood.'

'That's horrible!' Speck said and Oran gave a solemn nod.

'Thrugg was built to fight, but Thrugg doesn't want to fight,' said Thrugg.

'But what happened to the princess?' Speck asked.

The captain pursed his lips. 'The princess and Thrugg became friends.'

'Princess Juni was kind to Thrugg.' The gladiator nodded in thought.

'Aye. Juni, that was her name,' said Oran. 'One day, Juni and Thrugg hatched a plan to escape the horrors of the fighting pits. They had a dream to explore the expanse of the Galaxy, side by side.'

'But it didn't end up going that way,' said Nephora

who, having heard the tale many times before, couldn't help but join in.

'Alas, no,' said Oran. 'The pair were discovered on the eve of their escape. Thrugg, being the kind soul he is, sacrificed himself so that Juni could escape. The princess got away but Thrugg didn't. He was recaptured and dragged back to the fighting pits. After that day he refused to ever fight again. Eventually the slave owners grew tired of trying to force him to battle and he was sold to new owners. A few purchases later he came into my service as my personal bodyguard.'

'And Princess Juni?' Speck asked, mouth dry with anticipation.

Oran shook his head. 'No one knows. Thrugg stays by my side and he hopes that one day he might find his friend again. We all do.'

Speck looked to the lumbering beast, humbled by his tragic tale, and saw the gladiator in a new light. Thrugg was staring into the electric fire, a tear trickling down the raw flesh of his cheek. He might look like a fearsome monstrosity, Speck thought, but there was a big heart within that chest.

'I hope you find her again someday, Thrugg,' said Speck, and the gladiator looked at him with a sad smile.

'Thrugg hopes so too, little human.'

'So, as you can see, we're a truly miserable bunch to be around, kid.' Captain Oran winked.

'And what about you, Captain?' Speck ventured, realising there was one tale yet to be heard.

But the captain merely shook his head as a mysterious expression fell across his face.

'Not tonight,' he said. 'We've heard enough sad stories for one evening. Especially when we're in such a dire situation ourselves.'

The conversation died down and the pirates fell silent as they listened to the strange, alien sounds of the mysterious planet on which they had found themselves. After a while, Captain Oran got to his feet and wandered out to the edge of the marshy clearing, closely followed by Thrugg.

'I suppose the captain's story is even sadder than Thrugg's,' Speck said to Nephora. The Ureyan followed his gaze out to where the mighty captain stood, staring out into the dense fog.

'I wouldn't know,' she said with a shrug. 'He's never told us his story. He's a mystery, our Cappin'. As mysterious as this planet, I'd wager.'

Speck frowned.

'Here's a word of advice, kid,' said Randall, lowering his voice. 'Captain Oran may seem like a nice guy, but don't be fooled. You don't get to be the captain of a pirate crew by being kind-hearted.'

'What do you mean?' asked Speck, and Randall raised an eyebrow.

'Just be careful. That's what I mean. The captain's meaner than he lets on. He told you why that lumbering fool sticks around with him, but he didn't say why he purchased old Thrugg in the first place, did he? Thrugg is insistent that he'll find his dear princess one day, and the captain certainly hopes he will.'

'I'm sure he does,' replied Speck, confused. He looked over quizzically at Nephora and Quilch, but the pair had both suddenly found the ground much more interesting to look at.

'Aye, he hopes Thrugg finds the princess all right,' continued Randall. 'But not so they can have their big happy reunion. No, when the princess escaped from Thrakkush a bounty was put out for her return. A big reward for anyone that can bring her back. The only reason the captain keeps that lug around is because he hopes that one day Thrugg will lead him straight to her.'

'And the bounty,' Speck finished, understanding dawning. He looked out at the captain and the gladiator, hardly able to believe what he was hearing. 'That can't be true. The captain wouldn't betray his friend like that.'

Randall's eyes narrowed. 'The captain is less trustworthy than a Glunderon stinkrat in my humble opinion.'

Speck felt instantly troubled. He wanted to ask Nephora what she thought, but at that moment the captain came striding back to the camp and the pirates fell silent.

'You all had better get some rest,' he said. 'Tomorrow will be a long day.'

His gaze fell upon Speck and he frowned. 'Speck, are you all right? You look spooked.'

Speck's spine tingled as he stared at the ground.

'I'm fine, Captain,' he mumbled.

'Good,' Oran replied. 'Because you're part of this crew until we get off this rock, understand?'

Speck nodded.

'Now, get some rest, all of you. And that's an order.'

The pirates mumbled a chorus of 'aye, sir', and started to rise, following the captain back towards the ship.

Randall and Speck were the last to head in, and as Speck walked towards the ship, the navigator passed close enough to whisper to him.

'I'll look out for you, kid,' he said. 'Don't you worry. Just give me your word that when the time comes, I'll have your support.'

'Support for what?' Speck whispered back.

'You'll see,' said the navigator. His lips curled, his golden teeth glittering in the dying light and an unmistakable hunger in his dark eyes.

10

The Shriekers

Speck woke early the next morning following a restless night's sleep. As he lay awake in his storage shelf, brain ticking over, he'd come to the conclusion that he should prove himself as a member of the pirate crew. If the pirates needed a cook, then he'd be the best cook they could ever ask for. He figured that cooking couldn't be all that difficult anyway. On the Grand Orbital Library, he'd often been assigned kitchen duties, and though those duties usually consisted of doing little jobs such as helping whisk batter or chop vegetables, he'd seen enough to at least give it a go.

But Speck's dreams were quickly dashed when he discovered that the *Dawnchaser*'s kitchens were all but empty.

'How do you cook with no ingredients?' he asked Nuis despondently. The security drone didn't have an answer for him, and Speck tried the empty cupboards once more, just in case they'd magically filled up since the last time he'd checked.

'This is useless,' he said, but then his eyes lit up. 'Maybe there are ingredients outside we can use!'

Nuis blooped a warning, but it was too late. Speck was already leaving.

Speck opened the exterior hatch and jumped down onto the spongy moss of the mysterious planet. The mist had cleared since the night before and it seemed that Nephora had been right when she'd predicted that they were in the middle of a swamp. All around was thick foliage interspersed by large pools of stinking water and squelching mud.

'What a strange place,' Speck marvelled as he padded out into the clearing.

Nuis blooped cautiously and followed closely as Speck wandered through a line of thick trees, stooping low to avoid the purple branches coated in thick, sticky sap.

Speck squelched through the mire, climbed a steep hill, and soon found that he could see for kilometres in all directions. He stared out in wonder. A misty sea of alien red trees stretched out towards the horizon. The only other landmark to interrupt the view was a cluster of mountains in the far distance, their snow-laden peaks reflecting the shine of the nearest star.

'Do you think there's anything out there worth eating?' Speck asked Nuis.

Bleep! Nuis gave out a sharp, almost angry bloop

and Speck looked up to the drone with a frown.

'Well, there's no need to be so dramatic,' grumbled Speck. 'I was only asking.'

But Speck realised that the drone wasn't even listening to him. It was looking out towards the horizon, eye flashing red. Speck followed the drone's intense gaze.

'What is it?' Speck asked, scanning the horizon.

Then he saw what had grabbed the drone's attention and his breath caught.

There, within the swirls of the mist, was a distant dot. No, more than a dot. It was a silhouette.

But the figure wasn't walking. It was floating through the air, and Speck knew only one creature in the Galaxy who could levitate like that.

'The Starchild! It's here!' Speck gasped, turning to his drone companion. 'Can you record this, Nuis?'

Nuis bleeped haughtily as if to say, 'Of course I can.'

'We haven't lost it after all,' said Speck, relief flooding him. 'But look, it's heading away from us.'

It was true. The Starchild was getting further away from the hill Speck was standing on, heading towards the snow-capped peaks in the distance, and it wasn't long before its small frame was swallowed whole by the swirling mists around the mountain's base.

'Come on, Nuis,' said Speck, scrambling to his feet. 'We have to show the others.'

Speck spun and started to skid back down the hill, Nuis bleeping erratically right behind him. The pair raced through the jungle, hardly caring for the squelching mud or stinking swamp waters. They arrived breathlessly back at camp in time to find the pirate crew already outside, warming themselves round the heater. Captain Oran looked up with surprise as Speck raced into the clearing, yelling at the top of his voice.

'We saw it! We saw the Starchild!' he shouted excitedly as he slopped through the mire.

'The Starchild?' said Randall, scanning the surrounding trees.

'Yes!' cried Speck, between gasping breaths. 'Show them, Nuis.'

The security drone flipped open its viewing screen and played the video it recorded on the hill.

'It's on this planet,' said Speck as the pirates watched. 'We have to follow it!'

'Whoa, kid.' Oran held up a placating hand. 'We have our own problems. I don't think we should be wasting time chasing after that thing.'

Speck felt his heart fall. He'd been so caught up in his own excitement that he hadn't even stopped to think whether the pirates would want to help him.

'Then me and Nuis will just have to go and find it on our own,' said Speck stubbornly, though it was a scary thought going into the jungle with only Nuis for company.

Oran held out his hands. 'Not so fast,' he said. 'You're part of my crew while we're on this planet. You don't get to go out on your own unless I command it.'

Speck's heart sank even further and he felt anger begin to bubble away inside him. It was unfair. He would never have agreed to becoming part of the pirate crew if he'd known the Starchild was so close.

Quilch began to twitter thoughtfully and the crew nodded as they listened.

'I was wondering the same thing, Quilch,' the captain said. 'Why is the Starchild even here in the first place?'

'It must have a reason,' said Randall.

'That might explain why the black hole spat us out at such a precise location,' mused Nephora. 'This Starchild must have been using it as a tunnel through space, and we accidentally hitched a ride along with it. Just our luck.'

'Whatever the reason, it will have to remain a mystery,' said Oran with a tone of finality in his voice. 'We're staying as far away from that thing as possible.'

Speck felt tears of frustration building in his eyes. He couldn't believe it. He was so close but still so far away.

But then Thrugg, who had been silent up to that moment, rumbled as he shifted his immense weight, glancing down at the captain.

'Thrugg wonder . . . if space child can teleport Thrugg and friends here, then maybe space child can teleport Thrugg and friends back again?'

'Thrugg has a point,' said Nephora, her skin glimmering yellow for a moment. 'If this planet is as lacking in technology as it seems, then the Starchild could be our only chance of getting off this rock. We're not exactly going to stumble across a rallium store in the middle of a swamp.'

'Ridiculous!' Randall mocked. 'Are we supposed to merely ask it to drop us off home? Maybe it can make us a packed lunch for the journey too?'

'Thrugg will make space child agree,' Thrugg rumbled, clenching a humungous fist.

The captain bit his lip as he thought.

'You can't be considering it, Captain,' Randall said. 'Remember what happened last time we listened to one of the kid's ideas?'

'I do,' Oran said, his mind seemingly made up. 'And the only reason we're still alive is because of his quick thinking. All right Speck, we'll pursue the Starchild. Now, which way did you say it was going?'

Twenty minutes later, after a hasty breakfast, the pirates packed supplies and set off from their ship towards the distant mountains. The going was arduous, with the squelching mire making every step a monumental effort, but the pirates were motivated by their one chance of escaping the lost planet. It wasn't long before the grimly-determined crew were approaching the slopes of the distant mountains. As they drew nearer, a mournful wailing sound began to rise above the regular cacophony of the jungle, growing louder as they walked. The pirates all wore looks of fearful apprehension on their faces as they emerged from the jungle and came out onto the edge of a vast chasm that separated the jungle from the slopes of the mountain.

The chasm was like a huge scar cut into the planet's surface and Speck swiftly realised that the ferocious noise wasn't the call of some horrifying monster but was instead the sound of a powerful gale howling down the canyon itself, channelled by the rocky precipice.

And there, stretching across the wide chasm, was a sight none of the pirates had expected to see: an ancient metal bridge, held aloft by heavily eroded struts that wobbled wildly in the harsh winds. On the side of the bridge closest to them was a ramshackle guardhouse, overgrown with vines, and on the opposite side was the opening of an ominous cave carved into the mountainside.

'I'll be damned.' Nephora shook her head. 'Maybe this planet isn't as uncivilised as we thought.'

'If the Starchild was heading this way, then my money's on it having gone in there,' said the captain, pointing across the bridge at the dark cave.

'But how in the Galaxy do you plan to get us across?' asked a bewildered Randall. The wind looked strong enough to pluck even the bravest soul straight off the bridge and into the chasm below.

'I don't know,' conceded Oran. 'But there must be something around here that can help us. Spread out and look around.'

The pirates nodded and fanned out, making sure to stay sheltered from the howling wind as they hunted. Before long, the sound of Quilch's excited twittering was echoing out from within the abandoned guardhouse.

The pirates piled into the derelict shack to find the Quilkin standing by a set of mouldy lockers. Quilch was gesturing at a pair of heavy-looking boots sitting at the bottom of one of the lockers. On the sole of each was a long smooth sheet of metal and each boot was attached to a glove by a length of wire.

'He says they're called clamper boots,' Oran said, translating the Quilkin's excited chirps. 'Apparently they used them all the time in the asteroid mines. They're magnetic so you can stick to metal surfaces.'

'And there are switches in the gloves to turn the magnets on and off,' marvelled Nephora.

'We can use them to cross the bridge then,' said Oran with relief. 'Spread out and see if there are any more.'

The pirates did as they were bid and soon they had gathered another three pairs of the boots. Oran decided that three pairs were enough. Thrugg was far too heavy to be affected by the wind and Quilch would just have to be carried.

After donning the boots, the nervous pirates stood in line fidgeting.

'Ready everyone?' Captain Oran called.

'Nuis, you'd better stay inside my jumpsuit if you don't want to get blown away,' said Speck, unzipping the suit a little to make room for the drone.

'We ready,' Thrugg called from the back, Quilch cradled within the gladiator's sturdy arms. The captain gave a curt nod and began leading the ragtag crew out of the guardhouse and out onto the eroding bridge.

Speck took the first few steps to get used to the clamper boots. At first, he was terrified of getting the controls wrong and accidentally turning off both magnets, but after a few practice steps he got used to manipulating the controls.

The whipping wind was relentless as it tried to wrench him free from his boots and he was forced to lower his head just to shield his eyes from the intense gale. When he did finally look up again, he was shocked to find that Thrugg and Randall had both overtaken him and the captain and Nephora were already nearing the bridge's halfway point. He gasped and put his head down again. He'd have to put in extra effort to make sure he wasn't the last one to the other side.

Speck was concentrating on speeding up his marching when a shrieking sound suddenly blasted both his ears.

SHREEEEIIIAAK!

A flitting dark shadow whipped past Speck's face, gone again in an instant. He blinked, stunned, and glanced around, searching for the shadow, but there was nothing before him other than the wind.

I must have imagined it, he thought with a nervous laugh as he released the magnet on his right boot and prepared to take another step forward.

SHREEEEIIIAAK!

Another dark shadow whipped past his face. This time he was sure he hadn't imagined it.

'AGH!' came a sharp cry of disgust from up ahead. Speck glanced up to see Nephora, her eyes wide with terror as she wrestled with one of the shrieking shapes. The flittering shade convulsed as it clung tightly to the Ureyan. Finally, with a yell of anger, she flung the creature away, sending it flying onto one of the bridge's few surviving railings. At last Speck could see it properly. It was a large, slimy bug with leathery skin, veiny wings, and writhing tentacles, each lined with razor sharp teeth. Speck felt a shiver fall down his spine.

'Everybody go!' roared the captain.

Speck didn't need to be told twice. Putting his head down, he tried to concentrate on walking faster, but his panic made him falter with the controls. His breathing grew quicker and he was all too aware that he had only made it halfway across the bridge.

Carried by the wind, another three black shapes whizzed past his face.

Oof!

One of the bugs barrelled into his chest, snatching the air from his lungs. Its fang-lined tentacles latched onto his arms, sharp teeth cutting into his skin. Speck winced with pain and at the same moment a panic-stricken bleep sounded from under his chin. He glanced down to be met with Nuis' eye poking out from his jumpsuit, flashing in panic. The drone was trapped and the shrieker on Speck's chest was hovering above it, ready to strike.

'Get off!' Speck cried through gritted teeth, and he aimed a flailing punch at the bug. A wave of disgust passed through him as his fist made contact with the creature's slimy wet skin, but it was enough. With a startled hiss, its tentacles were ripped free and the bug was instantly snatched away by the wind.

Nuis gave a momentary bloop of relief, nestling back into the safety of the jumpsuit.

Just then, laser fire sounded from ahead and Speck glanced up to see that the other pirates had all but made it to the far side. Nephora, Randall and the captain were already under the shelter of the cavern, aiming laser blasters into the sky as more of the marauding bugs flew in, swept along on the gale. Thrugg was only a few steps away from sanctuary, the small figure of Quilch still cradled in his arms.

'Come on, Speck!' Oran called to him. 'Keep moving!'

Speck nodded, gritting his teeth and trying to

control his panic. Remember, he told himself. It's easy. Left switch, left foot. Right switch, right foot.

But his body was refusing to obey his thoughts and the air was getting thicker with the creatures. His view of the pirates at the cavern's mouth was fast becoming obscured by the swarm of black shapes.

Suddenly, he felt an intense burning pain in his arm as another of the creatures collided into him. And then a second and a third. His view was completely obscured by buzzing wings and he batted manically at them with flailing hands.

A series of loud bloops emerged from within Speck's jumpsuit and he realised that Nuis was trapped too, just as helpless as he was.

This is it, thought Speck. This is the end of my big adventure.

But then, just as suddenly, Speck felt the tentacles of the shriekers being ripped away from his skin. He looked up to see Thrugg standing there. The gladiator had dropped Quilch off before coming back for him! Thrugg was swarming with the vile creatures, but despite the bites on his flesh he was only concerned with plucking the blood-sucking beasts from Speck's startled frame.

'Speck turn boots off!' Thrugg bellowed over the wind.

Speck understood. He flicked his magnetic boots off and before he knew it Thrugg had grabbed him with his immense hands. Holding Speck to his chest,

Thrugg turned and charged toward the cavern on the far side of the bridge.

Speck lashed out at as many of the creatures as he could but before long all he could see were black shapes. He felt Thrugg's charge beginning to slow. The hundreds of shriekers were too heavy even for him.

Tears began bubbling in Speck's eyes as Thrugg slowed to a standstill. He could hear the giant's laboured breaths and he realised the gladiator wasn't able to defend himself with his arms full.

'You have to let me go, Thrugg!' Speck pleaded. 'You have to fight them!'

But the gladiator wouldn't listen and Speck couldn't even see the cave past the thick throng of shriekers. Somewhere beneath the screeching creatures and the howling wind, Speck could make out the voices of the crew calling to them.

'Thrugg!' cried Captain Oran desperately. 'Over here!'

'I throw you,' rumbled Thrugg, between his grunts of pain.

'Throw me?' Speck cried. 'You can't!'

'Good luck, friend Speck,' Thrugg rumbled. 'Me hope you find star kid.' Before Speck could protest any more, he was hurtling through the air. The world was toppling, spinning past his vision like a blur, and he hit the ground sharply. Speck wheezed, his bones ached, but he realised that he'd made it. The cavern roof was above him and he no longer felt the wind mercilessly whipping at his body.

'Thrugg!' The captain was still calling out to his bodyguard. Speck picked himself up from the floor to see the gladiator only a few metres from the lip of the cave, roaring in anger as he fired his many weapons at the attacking shriekers. The air was lit with lasers and flames as the gladiator defended himself. Countless numbers of the bloodsuckers fell away, but just as many continued to pile onto the gladiator's body, and then the weight was too much for Thrugg. The gladiator was sliding towards the bridge's edge. 'Thrugg! No!' Captain Oran ran to help, but Randall put out a hand, grabbing the captain's shoulder.

'No, Captain! You'll just be swept away too!' cried the navigator.

Thrugg was now completely covered by the shriekers. Speck's breath caught in his throat. Tears filled his eyes. The world hung for a horrible moment. The gladiator teetered on the bridge's edge.

Then, in a cloud of swirling black shapes, Thrugg was pushed off. The gladiator's deep-set eyes widened in a mix of surprise and fear as he tumbled from the bridge. His mournful wail echoed as he dropped into the depths of the chasm below.

11

Double Deception

Captain Oran crumpled to the ground, his eyes wide.

'Thrugg,' he whispered. Outside, the black shriekers continued to whip past the cavern entrance in a blinding swarm. Speck glanced round at the other pirates, standing open-mouthed and unable to believe what had just happened. All except Randall, that was, who wore a thin smile on his crooked lips.

Speck could hardly comprehend it. The gladiator was gone. Just like that.

'Can't we do something?' he asked in a small voice.

'There's nothing we can do,' Nephora said quietly.

'But, but –' stammered Speck. It was impossible. There had to be something they could do; he just had no idea what that something was.

'Captain?' Nephora nudged gently. The captain was staring at the spot where the gladiator had stood only moments before.

'He can't be gone,' whispered Oran.

'Captain, I'm sorry but we need to keep moving,' pressed Nephora, moving to put a hand on Oran's shoulder.

'Don't touch me!' the captain snapped. Nephora's eyes widened and her skin flushed blue.

'Sorry,' the captain said, shaking his head. 'Please, I need to be alone for a moment.'

Nephora looked at the other pirates searchingly and Randall took the moment to step forward.

'If the captain is too preoccupied to get us out of this mess, then I suppose it falls to this humble navigator to take the lead.'

Speck looked imploringly at the captain, but it was true. The great man was too engulfed in despair to even notice.

'Take a look around,' Randall ordered, enjoying his temporary command. 'Stay together and keep your lasers handy. This Starchild could be anywhere.'

Speck nodded, his heart heavy as he turned his attention to the interior of the cavern.

'Look at him,' said Randall as they walked out of earshot of their captain. 'Crying over his lost reward. Pathetic.'

'I don't know,' Speck whispered back. 'I think he's really sad about losing Thrugg.'

Randall only scoffed. 'I'll tell you for the last time, there's only one thing that a pirate cares for and it isn't friends or family. It's gold.'

Then maybe I'm not cut out to be a pirate,

thought Speck bitterly, as the pirates ventured into the humungous chamber, but he held his tongue.

The cavern was pitch black, but with a bloop, Nuis brightened its eye, lighting the way. The cave was expansive and evidently long abandoned. Large, purple mushrooms coated the rocky walls, dripping viscous pools of slime onto the floor and Speck was forced to sidestep some goop at the very last second as it dripped down from above. All across, the chamber was strewn with abandoned crates of supplies, left to collect dust.

'What do you think is behind those doors?' Speck asked, pointing to the far end of the cavern where two heavy, dust-coated metal doors stood. They were shut and marked with a crude symbol, the likes of which Speck had never seen before.

'I wouldn't have a clue,' said Randall. 'This whole planet is rather an irritating mystery.'

Quilch tweeted his agreement. Speck was half expecting Thrugg to add his voice to proceedings and felt a lump form in his throat when he realised that he would never hear the gladiator's gentle rumble again.

'Let's spread out,' Randall ordered. 'Maybe we'll find a way to open that door.'

The pirates split up. Only Speck hesitated. He turned back towards the cave's entrance, where the captain was still seated cross-legged at the edge of the cave's mouth.

With a sigh, Speck ambled back and sat down beside the captain. He wasn't sure how to console any human being – let alone a fearsome pirate captain. He couldn't mention Thrugg, that was for sure. He was positive that any mention of the gladiator would only make the captain sadder. But then again, maybe not.

When Speck was first brought to the Orbital Library, when he was very young, he had become fast friends with an unlikely utility bot called V-Z. Speck's playmate was a much older model of robot than the rest of the droids. In fact, he had been the last remaining bot of his production line. Because of this, V-Z had always been somewhat of an outcast. 'Quirky' is how the other bots described him and it was undoubtedly this that drew Speck to him. But as time wore on, the parts used to replenish V-Z were no longer manufactured. They became rarer to obtain and after an incident in the engine room one fateful evening, there were no more parts left with which to renew the bot's ailing body.

Speck couldn't remember V-Z too well now. It was long ago, after all, but when he thought about his old friend, he didn't feel sad. He only felt the overwhelming sense of love that he had known for the bot.

Thrugg should be remembered too, Speck thought resolutely, and he turned to Captain Oran. 'Thrugg was a real hero.'

'He was more than just a hero,' said the captain quietly. 'He was a friend and a guardian and . . .' Oran shook his head. 'Never mind,' said the pirate. 'He's gone now.'

'It was my fault,' admitted Speck. 'I should have been quicker crossing the bridge.'

Speck expected the captain to be angry with him, but instead Oran had a soft smile on his lips.

'Not at all, Speck,' said the captain. 'It was always Thrugg's choice to help those in need. You shouldn't feel to blame.'

'Randall said that pirates only care about gold. He said they don't care about things like friends.'

'Aye,' said Oran thoughtfully. 'If that's true then perhaps Thrugg wasn't a very good pirate, after all.'

Speck frowned. He was about to bring up the subject of the Thrakkush bounty, but before he could, a shout of excitement arose from the far end of the cavern. Speck and the captain both looked around to find Randall dancing with excitement under Nuis' glowing eye.

'We're saved!' cackled the navigator. 'Saved!'

'What have you found?' Nephora asked, as the pirates all raced to see.

'Don't thank me all at once,' Randall said as he pointed. Nuis directed its torchlight onto a silent hovercraft sitting in the gloom. It was old and covered in dust, but otherwise in one piece.

'A hovercraft,' Nephora marvelled.

'It still works,' Randall said. 'But that's not all. Look at what's sitting in the crate next to it.'

Randall pointed again and Nuis dutifully illuminated the open container sitting beside the hovercraft. Within sat several glowing tubes that pulsed with a gently ebbing light.

Nephora's eyes lit up. 'Rallium. It's rallium! We can refuel the ship and get off this planet. We're saved!'

The pirates fell into thankful cheering, except for the captain.

'If only Thrugg could have held on a little longer,' said Oran quietly and Speck grasped the captain's hand gently.

'Yes, quite,' murmured Randall, clearing his throat. 'It is such a shame that blithering oaf isn't around anymore.'

The captain's eyes widened and his face flooded crimson with rage. 'Watch your mouth.'

Speck felt his hand clench.

'Or what?' Randall smiled. 'What will you do now that your humble bodyguard isn't here to fight your battles for you?'

'I can fight my own battles,' the captain said quietly, menacingly. His hand fell to where his blaster was, except – it wasn't there. He froze.

Randall's grin widened. 'Oh dear. Is your blaster missing? You should know by now that one of the skills our Quilkin friend mastered in the great asteroid

mines was how to pick pockets rather effectively.'
Randall pointed his blaster directly at the captain.
Next to him stood Quilch, clasping the captain's
own weapon, a devilish grin on the Quilkin's bird-
like features.

'What are you doing?' demanded the captain,
taking half a step back. 'This is mutiny.'

'I suppose it is.' Randall's face hardened. 'We're
quite fed up with your leadership and I'm rather
enjoying being in command myself. I don't think I'll
be handing it back anytime soon.'

'You can't just decide to be captain,' said Nephora
tensely. 'We won't let you.'

'Oh, I think you will,' Randall said. 'Once you
know what I know.'

Nephora frowned, looking from the captain to
Speck. 'What's he talking about, Cappin'?'

But the captain was only glaring at Randall, fury
burning in his eyes.

'I always wondered about you,' Randall said
nonchalantly. 'You seemed such a mystery. Nobody
knows a thing about who you are, or where you came
from. I had my suspicions, but it wasn't until today
that they were confirmed.'

Speck looked from Oran to Randall, utterly lost.

'I've been biding my time, you see,' continued
Randall. 'Waiting for the moment that doting dolt
of yours let his guard down, but he never did. Then
today came, and now your old friend Thrugg is

out of the picture. If you can recall, I was the one who stopped you from going back out to help him.' Randall was truly enjoying himself now, his eyes glowing with malice as he spoke to his captivated audience. 'I was the one who put a hand on your shoulder and held you back from joining Thrugg on the bridge. Just to make sure.'

The captain's eyes widened. 'No,' he gasped.

'Yep!' Randall looked to the rest of the pirates. 'When I put my hand on the captain's shoulder, I learnt something rather interesting. You see, there's a reason Thrugg never let anyone touch a hair on the captain's head.' His eyes fell back onto the captain. 'Show them.'

'Never,' growled Oran.

'Very well then.'

Randall held up his blaster, pulled the trigger and shot Captain Oran in the chest.

Speck cried out. Nephora's mouth fell open. Quilch twittered and Randall stood firm, waiting.

The smoke from the laser blast cleared. Captain Oran was clutching his chest. Except he wasn't Captain Oran anymore. All around him a blue light was glimmering and fading. His appearance was changing before their eyes and Speck realised that Randall hadn't shot the captain at all. Instead, he had shot a computer console hidden on the captain's chest. Already the hologram around Oran's body was flickering and fading as the console died.

Speck gasped. A phantom suit! Randall had shot the suit's control panel and the hologram had failed. There in front of him, where the captain had stood moments before, was a young girl, tall for her age but hardly older than Speck. She had dark skin and white hair. Her face was hard-set and her jaw clenched in fury.

'Captain Oran,' said Randall, bowing mockingly. 'Or should I call you by your real name, Princess Juni?'

Nephora's face had fallen and she was shaking her head in disbelief. The princess looked between the crew members. Her face was contorted in anger, but Speck could see the fear brimming in her eyes. He was speechless. He didn't know what to think, but everything was falling into place too swiftly. He understood now how the captain had been so quick to realise that Speck had been wearing a phantom suit of his own on Calestine. He understood why Thrugg was so desperate to stop anyone going near his beloved captain.

Randall's eyes narrowed. 'You were never separated from Thrugg at all, were you? The story was all true, except for that small detail. I have to admit, it was clever – but unfortunately for you, I'm smarter.'

Princess Juni glared. 'I'm still your captain. No matter what I look like. It changes nothing.' Her voice still came out as deep as Oran's had been.

Speck noticed a small box attached to the side of her neck, no longer camouflaged and blinking whenever she talked.

'A voice disguiser,' said the navigator. 'Very clever.' He waltzed across to the princess and plucked the box from Juni's throat.

'No!' she snapped, her disguised voice eradicated.

'You lied to us,' spat Nephora. Her skin had flushed a deep crimson. 'All this time you've been playing us for fools. We'll be the laughing stock of the Galaxy if it gets out we've been led by a kid this whole time.'

'Aye,' murmured Randall. 'But it could also make us rich.'

Nephora looked to Randall.

'I suggest we make a small change to our plans,' said the navigator. 'Elect me captain and we'll use this hovercraft to transport the rallium back to the ship. Then we can set a course straight for Thrakkush and collect the reward for the princess ourselves.'

'You can't!' Speck blurted, aghast.

'We can,' replied Nephora, her skin still glowing blood red as her anger rose. 'It's about time we made some money.'

Randall turned to Speck. 'What did I try and tell you, kid? A pirate's allegiance is to gold. Now, what about you? Are you with us, or against us?'

Speck looked from the pirates to the captive princess who had moments before been Captain Oran. Juni's head was hung and he could see her blinking back furious tears.

'You can be anything you want to be,' Vargel Pren had once said.

He didn't want to be this.

'Against you,' he said, through gritted teeth.

'Alas,' sighed Randall. 'How tragic. But it hardly matters. More gold for us!'

The pirates cheered and Randall gestured the others toward the hovercaft.

'Quilch, get this craft up and running,' he ordered. 'Vart, kindly escort our captive on board.'

'Aye, Cappin',' said Nephora as she levelled her laser blaster at the princess.

'You can't do this!' Speck spat. He didn't know what to do. He was powerless. He'd thought the pirates were his friends. Not only that, but without them he'd never have a chance of finding the Starchild, let alone getting off the planet. Speck felt tears brimming.

'Leave her alone!' he cried.

'It's okay, kid,' the princess said. Her anger had been swallowed and she looked defeated as Nephora pushed her toward the hovercraft. 'Looks like you're not a pirate after all. And neither was I.'

Speck continued to protest, but the pirates ignored him, and soon Quilch had the hovercraft up and running. It hummed and whined as its long-dormant engines ignited, rising unsteadily into the air.

'It's a tough break,' Randall said as he waved to

Speck and leapt onto the hovercraft, the crate of rallium under his arm. 'No hard feelings. You can't blame a pirate for being a pirate!'

Randall spat phlegm, and Speck could only watch as the craft rose high into the air, kicking up dust and mushroom slime. Speck covered his ears and the craft rushed by. It rocketed out of the cave's entrance and Speck was alone once more.

12

Secrets of the Lost Planet

'What am I going to do, Nuis?' Speck was standing at the mouth of the cavern, staring in the direction to which the pirates had recently departed.

His mind was still reeling over the fact that Captain Oran had never existed. No matter how dire his own situation was, he couldn't help but feel sorry for Princess Juni. Not only had she lost her best friend, but also her crew – all in the space of ten minutes. Yet she'd hardly shed a tear when the pirates had taken her away.

If Princess Juni could be strong, then he could be too. He might still be able to help her. But even if he wanted to help the princess, what could he do? He'd thought about heading back across the bridge – he still had his clamper boots – but even if he got past the shriekers, the pirates would be long gone by the time he arrived back at the ship.

Nuis suddenly gave out a short, sharp beep of despair.

'What's wrong, Nuis?'

The drone blooped, but the noise sounded distant and slurred.

'Your battery's running low?' Speck guessed nervously. 'You'd better switch to low-power mode.'

Nuis nodded, dimming its eye light.

Speck quickly squashed down the panic bubbling inside of him. No matter what had happened with the pirates, he'd come here on a mission to find the Starchild, and he had to follow through with it. Now he just had to work out where the Starchild had gone before Nuis ran out of battery. Simple.

Speck turned back to the cave and his eyes fell on the two sturdy doors at the end of the chamber. Maybe the Starchild had gone deeper into the cavern. He approached the doors. They were completely smooth, with no apparent handles and no computer console to operate them.

'Just our luck,' he mumbled to Nuis.

Speck stood back, folding his arms. Despite it all, there was something very familiar about the symbol scrawled on the front of the doors. The odd marking consisted of a 'V' shape situated within a circle.

'Odd,' he mused out loud to Nuis. 'Where have I seen something like that?'

Then it clicked. He had seen a very similar symbol before, scrawled on Yabba's chest.

'Gutterlings!' Speck cried out. 'It's the sign of a Gutterling tribe!'

Nuis gave a quizzical bloop.

'Look,' said Speck, pointing. 'It's just like the symbol for the Gumu tribe – only some of the lines are different. This mark must belong to a different tribe.'

It must mean something, he thought to himself. He had been pronounced a friend to all Gutterlings. If only he could remember the words that Yabba had taught him.

'What were the words?' he pondered aloud to Nuis. He still couldn't remember!

Your head is always in the clouds, his mother-bot would have scorned him.

You're too distracted to focus on your studies, the Keepers would have tutted at him. He always tried so hard, but just for once he wished he could focus.

'Chimi . . .'

Nuis' light began to fade a little more and it blooped in a mournful manner.

'Chimi . . . choro . . .'

He pictured Yabba's lips pronouncing the three words.

'Chimi . . . choro . . . yoko!' he called out, surprising even himself.

That was it! He was sure of it!

'Chimi choro yoko!' he yelled out at the top of his voice, and then once again for good measure, 'Chimi choro yoko!'

There was silence. Nuis' torchlight finally flickered

out and Speck was plunged into darkness.

'Oh no,' he whispered.

But then, with a sharp crack, the two doors began to open, creaking and whining as they went. Light poured through from beyond and Speck was greeted by a long grey corridor lit by fluorescent lamps. Not only that. There, standing in the doorway, was the unmistakable figure of a Gutterling.

'Welcome, stranger,' croaked the being, and Speck realised this Gutterling was ancient. Her fur was wispy and grey and one of her eyes was covered with an eyepatch. Her back was bent at such an angle that Speck was worried it might snap at any moment.

'Thank you,' Speck said, surprised that the Gutterling could speak his language.

'Nom does not know stranger's face,' said the elderly being. 'But the words stranger speaks mean that he is friend of Gumu tribe, yes?'

Speck nodded vigorously. 'The great scientist Yabba taught me those words himself.'

'Very good,' replied the rickety being, with the faintest of smiles. 'I be Nom of the Ogga tribe. Nice it is to meet you, friend of Gumu tribe.'

Speck hurriedly introduced himself, as well as Nuis. The drone blooped drunkenly as its eye lit up for a second.

'Friend sounds very unwell,' Nom murmured, casting a cautious eye upon Nuis.

'He's almost run out of power,' Speck explained, patting his friend gently.

'Then Speck and friend are most fortunate that they have arrived here.'

Without another word, Nom gestured for the pair to follow and began retreating down the corridor at a startlingly fast pace. Speck hurriedly took hold of Nuis and carefully nestled him in his jumpsuit before following the elderly Gutterling.

'Nom,' said Speck, as he followed the surprisingly speedy being. 'If you don't mind me asking, where exactly is "here"?'

'Speck does not know?' Nom said, astonishment clear on her face. 'But why else would Speck come to planet, if not for coming here?'

'It was an accident really,' Speck told her, feeling a wave of sadness overcome him as he remembered the reality of his situation. 'You see, we're looking for a creature called the Starchild. I don't suppose you've seen it?'

'Starchild?' Nom repeated. 'Hmm, there was another visitor here before Speck, but other visitor came in without even asking permission. Appeared and disappeared again without care in Universe. Nom couldn't keep track. Much rude!'

Speck felt his heart race. He had been right; the Starchild had come here! But for what reason? And where had it gone now? Speck felt his chances of escaping the mysterious planet slipping away, but a small part of him was relieved. Just thinking about the Starchild's blazing eyes sent a shiver down his spine.

Belatedly, Speck realised that they'd reached the end of the corridor. Nom was holding open a door to a small chamber. Except for a second door at the far end, this new room appeared to contain nothing at all. Perplexed, Speck entered and Nom shut the door behind them, pressing a series of buttons on the wall.

'Hold arms up,' ordered the ancient Gutterling.

Speck did as requested and gave out a stark cry as he was suddenly sprayed from head to toe with a chilly liquid. Nuis gave out a bleep of surprise as it too was drenched.

'Apologies, little drone,' murmured Nom. 'But cleaning agent is necessity to keep laboratories spotless.'

'Laboratories?' echoed Speck.

'Mm, yes, laboratories,' said Nom, opening the second door in the chamber. 'Most top-secret laboratories these are. Only very lucky Ogga tribe work here. Now Nom is only one left. Nom keep laboratories clean while masters are away.'

They passed through the second door and Speck found himself amidst a series of pristine white corridors with windows that gave views into sterile laboratories. It reminded him of being back on board the Grand Orbital Library, and he could scarce believe that such a place existed under the surface of this miserable planet.

'Where on Varillis are we?' Speck blurted. 'I've never even heard of a planet like this.'

'Nom not surprised. This be the Lost Planet.'

'How can a planet be lost?' Speck asked curiously. 'Don't they stay more or less in the same place?'

'Not this one,' replied Nom. 'This planet always moving. Sometimes it be in one place in Galaxy, sometimes on opposite side completely. That why it a such good place for secret laboratory. Now, let us get to control room. We get you warm and get power for your friend.'

Nom led a confused Speck and Nuis through the corridors and to a large chamber. A vast monitor adorned one wall and before it sat a large bank of computers.

'Welcome to control room,' said Nom.

Nuis spotted a charging port by the computers and, with an excited bloop, floated across, latching on and sighing as electricity began flowing into its circuits.

Nom played the perfect host, fetching Speck a blanket and some soup from her own quarters. Speck felt his stomach gurgling with hunger as the elderly creature ambled back with a piping hot bowl of creamy broth.

'Nom always have mushroom soup on simmer,' explained the Gutterling. 'Lots of mushrooms in caves. Very nutritious. Normally smarty scientists don't allow Nom to eat in laboratory, but Nom is breaking rules when they not here.' She winked at Speck and grinned wickedly.

'Thank you, Nom,' said Speck, devouring the soup and soaking it all up with a hunk of fresh fungus bread. For a moment, both Speck and Nuis were content as they rested.

'Where is everyone, Nom?' Speck asked after he had finished draining his bowl and set it aside. 'Is it just you here?'

'It is,' sighed the being. 'Big experiment all finished for now, so everyone leave.'

'What was the experiment?'

Nom shrugged. 'Nom doesn't know. Nom not even allowed in control room when smarty scientists be here, except to clean it at night.'

So very mysterious, thought Speck. Yet the Starchild must have had a reason for coming to the secret laboratory. Speck peered round the pristine chamber. Maybe there was a clue to be found somewhere?

'Do these computers still work?' he asked Nom, striding across to them.

'Nom doesn't see why not,' she said. 'Power come from deep down in planet core.'

Speck pressed a key on one of the consoles. Immediately the large monitor sprang to life.

PASSWORD REQUIRED, the screen read.

It was locked. But a password had never stopped Speck before.

Reaching for his utility belt, he pulled out his console tablet and attached the terminal connectors.

Getting past the password was more difficult than opening the Starchild's cell, but after a few minutes of focused tinkering he managed to bypass it. He grinned as the screen turned green, thinking that even U-T would have been impressed by how fast he had cracked the security.

PASSWORD ACCEPTED, the screen read, and suddenly hundreds of computer files were flooding the screen.

Speck frowned, scanning the numerous files. They all looked like nonsense to him.

'What are all these?' he asked Nom, but the little Gutterling was just as perplexed.

Speck frowned and chose one of the files at random.

A recorded video suddenly popped up on the screen. In the video, a squat being was standing exactly where Speck was positioned at that very moment. The being had orange skin and small beady eyes hidden behind thick spectacles.

'Ah, it be head smarty scientist, Bizzabin,' said Nom. 'This must be Bizzabin video diary.'

'It is the fifth day of Quantanak,' spoke the being named Bizzabin from the screen, pushing his spectacles up the bridge of his large nose. 'My excitement is almost too much. Today we begin our latest experiment. My team has been tasked with the impossible. Our employer wishes us to condense and recreate the powers of the mighty space wyrm – those colossal creatures that are known to devour stars and create black holes. The boss wishes to know whether it could ever be possible to replicate such an extraordinary process. The only way to find out is to study the creatures themselves – a task which has until now been all but impossible. But with this new laboratory in place, we finally have a chance to discover the secrets of the space wyrm and I, Bizzabin, will go down in history as the greatest scientist of all time.'

The video file ended abruptly and Speck frowned. He selected another video file, further down the list. Again, Bizzabin's face popped up on the screen. This time the being had slight bags under both of his beady eyes.

'It is the thirtieth day of Quantanak,' Bizzabin reported with a tinge of exasperation.

'We are behind schedule, and the boss is displeased with our lack of progress. While we have been able to isolate the power of the space wyrm, the essence of star-eating is far too intense to be contained outside of a living host. We require a subject who is willing to be given the wyrm's fantastic power, but I believe such power could easily drive any being insane. I fear we will continue hitting this wall unless a drastic change is soon made.'

The video file ended once more and Speck felt a cold shiver passing through his body. He didn't like where this was heading. Regardless, he scrolled down the list of video diaries and selected another.

'Twenty-second day of Quirriek,' reported a very dishevelled-looking Bizzabin. 'Our gracious employer has somehow found a volunteer to undergo the trials. He is highly confident that the subject will be able to undertake the difficult process. But I was surprised to discover that this subject is merely a human child! He goes by the name of Ardulus, and I must admit, I am worried. The boy is only young, but our employer promises us that Ardulus is strong-willed and will not succumb to madness. I will report back when our young test subject arrives.'

Speck picked another file, his eyes glued to the screen.

'It is the twenty-fifth day of Quirriek and Ardulus has arrived,' reported a grinning Bizzabin. 'Ardulus is a courageous young being indeed! He hardly bats an eyelid when I tell him what trials must be undertaken. He is power-hungry, I can see it in his eyes. It is a hunger we share. My one concern is how he will react once the experiment is fully complete, but I believe, like our employer does, that Ardulus has the steel to come out of this process a being of much immense power!'

And another file.

'Thirty-fourth day of Quirriek,' enthused a beaming Bizzabin. 'Significant changes have occurred to young Ardulus since we infused him with the power of the space wyrm. He has transformed in appearance and is no longer recognisable as human. He complains of being hungry all the time but refuses to eat any food that we put before him. My hope is that what he hungers for is the flaming matter of a star. Then he truly will be akin to the mighty space wyrm! We will transport him to a nearby solar system next week so that he may feed.'

And another . . .

'Fourth day of Vastalan – and we have success! Ardulus' feeding trip went without a hitch and our employer is very pleased by our progress. Ardulus fed from the star, and as he did so a miraculous change came about his body. His eyes began to glow in a most intense manner. He believes that he can control when to release this power again. This is truly a miraculous turn of events and perhaps the happiest day of this humble scientist's life!'

Speck could hardly stop now. With fevered fingers he eagerly opened the next file. He was nearing the end of the list.

'Twelfth day of Vastalan. A near fatal accident occurred today,' reported Bizzabin. He seemed deflated. Speck could see scorch marks on the being's lab coat. 'I had, in the previous week, started observing worrisome changes in Ardulus. He no longer reacts to his own name and demands to be referred to only as "Starchild". I fear his memory is slowly fading and soon he may not even remember who he is. Yesterday, he confided in me that he has been conversing with something he calls "the void". I had originally put these rantings down to the stress placed upon his young shoulders, but I am becoming less sure of this by the day.

'Then, today, one of the laboratory assistants angered Ardulus when waking the boy for testing. Ardulus said that he didn't feel like participating in any trials and, in a fit of anger, released the energy stored in his body right here in the lab. What an explosion! Fortunately, we have prepared for this eventuality. Ardulus was contained before too much damage could occur.

'Still, it was worrying. Ardulus could have created a black hole right here in the lab and then we would have all been doomed. Nevertheless, the boss is pleased with these advances. We have all known from the beginning that this new science could be used for destructive purposes, but the boss is certain that such a weapon will bring a new era of peace to the Galaxy. Until we have a better understanding of the Starchild's powers, he has suggested keeping Ardulus better contained until further notice.'

And then the final file on the computer. Speck, with bated breath, opened it. Bizzabin was there, red-eyed and manic. He looked like he hadn't slept in days.

'Nineteenth day of Vastalan. Our employer has just informed me that he intends to take the Starchild away from our facility. He says that he has lost faith in my abilities and has instead made a deal with the High Librarian of the Grand Orbital Library. He will utilise the Night Eaters as well as the Library's laboratories to continue the research. Pah! Those useless bums are hardly scientists! I have it in mind to abandon my post here once he has taken the Starchild away. Maybe I'll sell my research on one of the outlaw moons. Then he'll see that nobody messes with Head Scientist Bizzabin!'

The video cut out. Silence reigned.

Speck couldn't believe what he had just seen. So the Starchild hadn't been born of the stars after all. He was a human boy, just like Speck. But what could have ever possessed Ardulus to want to volunteer to become the Starchild?

Speck's thoughts were suddenly interrupted by a sniffling noise behind him. An alarmed bloop sounded out from Nuis and Nom uttered a sharp gasp of her own. Speck turned – and froze.

There he was! No more than five metres away from Speck – hovering just above the floor.

The Starchild was right there.

His eyes were blazing with less fury than usual, and Speck could see a tear trickling down his leathery cheek. His eyes were focussed on the screen and Speck realised he must have been watching Bizzabin's reports from behind his back the whole time.

'I've been waiting,' said the Starchild finally, his voice burning through the air. 'You can't imagine how frustrated I was to arrive here after so long only to discover that the answers I was searching for were hidden behind a password. Despite all my powers I could not get past it. But then you came along and bypassed it in seconds.'

Speck gasped. He didn't know what to say.

'I found Bizzabin on Calestine,' continued the Starchild. 'He told me his story, but I couldn't believe it until I saw it with my own eyes. And so, I came here. Though I must admit I had no idea that I had been followed.'

'Ardulus . . .' Speck began.

'Do not call me that!' bellowed the Starchild, clenching his fists. The whole laboratory began shaking violently and Speck quickly shut his mouth.

'I am no longer that foolish boy,' the being continued. 'I did not lie to you on the night we first met. I told you I sought my parents. I desperately craved to know who I was and where I belonged in the Galaxy. And now I know. I am a monster.'

'But you don't have to be,' said Speck.

'Ha!' spat the Starchild. 'Don't be a fool. I was designed to be a weapon. I was designed to destroy.'

Speck bit his lip. Thrugg had also been designed to destroy, he thought, but he had never met a gentler creature.

'Now that I have returned to this place I am plagued by my old memories. They make me so – angry.'

'I know it's painful . . .' Speck began, but his words quickly petered out.

'Painful?' roared the Starchild. 'You have no idea who Ardulus was. You have no idea of my true pain.'

Speck frowned. He chanced a glance across to Nom, and then Nuis. Both were frozen in fear.

'I don't,' he admitted.

'Maybe it's better if I gave you my full name,' said the Starchild. 'You see, my full name is Ardulus Monk. That's right. The leader of the Night Eaters is my father, as well as the man who employed that scientist to create his super weapon. Do you see now? He volunteered his own son as a test subject. And I agreed to it. So desperate was I to win my father's approval, that I allowed myself to be turned into this!'

Speck couldn't believe his ears. His former hero, the formidable Giddius Monk, had transformed his own son into a . . . monster?

'And now,' said the Starchild, voice brimming with rage. 'I think it's time that I showed my father what he has created. It's time to prove to him what an unstoppable force I can be!'

And with that, the Starchild clicked his fingers and was gone, vanishing into thin air. Before Speck even knew what was happening, the entire room was shaking violently and he realised that it was collapsing around him.

13

The Star Eater

'You and your friend must leave now!' Nom demanded, already on her feet. 'Come, friend Speck – quickly.'

Speck didn't need telling twice. Nuis reluctantly abandoned its charging bay and the pair scrambled to follow Nom as she scampered back through the winding corridors. Already the lights were flickering and dust was trickling down from the ceiling as the planet threatened to cave in on itself.

'Faster, friend Speck!' cried the Gutterling.

The trio reached the sterilising chamber. Nom opened the first door and scuttled straight across to the exit.

'No time for cleaning,' she muttered. 'Oh, how it pains Nom, but no time!'

She opened the second door and the friends poured through. They sprinted down the corridor and had just reached the doors through to the cavern when Speck realised that Nom had come to a sudden stop.

'This is as far as Nom goes,' said the creature. 'Nom is sworn to look after secret laboratory, no matter what.'

'The laboratory won't exist soon!' Speck cried, but he could already tell that it didn't matter to the ancient Gutterling.

'Maybe it will. Maybe it won't. Either way, there will be lots of cleaning for Nom to do.' She rubbed her hands together merrily. 'Now, there is little time for arguing, friend Speck. You must stop this creature that smarty scientists create from destroying more planets!'

Speck nodded. He had to do something. He had to try.

He moved forward and embraced the little creature tightly, thinking, not for the first time, what noble beings Gutterlings were.

'Good luck, friend Speck!' Nom called, waving as she turned and scampered back down the corridor towards her beloved laboratory.

'Come on, Nuis,' Speck said breathlessly, and they sprinted for the mouth of the cavern. Outside the cave, the planet was truly being torn asunder. The wind howled. The trees of the jungle were being ripped clean from the ground and tossed high into the air. The very land seemed to be convulsing.

'What's happening?' Speck asked Nuis. How would he ever hope to get off the mysterious planet?

There has to be a way, he thought.

And then he saw it, far in the distance: a small shape rising up from the trees.

'Look, Nuis!' he said, pointing. 'The *Dawnchaser*! The pirates must have only just finished fuelling up.'

Nuis blooped excitedly.

'It's the only way off this planet,' Speck said. 'We have to get to that ship.'

But how? Speck looked round at the cavern despairingly, just as another boulder came crashing down beside him.

There was nothing for it. He turned to the bridge, about to activate his clamper boots, when –

'Whoa!' he felt a curious weightlessness come over his whole body and a blue glow illuminated around him.

With a startled gasp, he realised he was being lifted away from the ground. Craning his neck, he saw Nuis behind him, anti-grav net activated. The security drone blooped as if to say, 'Hang on', and suddenly Speck was rocketing forward, propelled in the anti-grav net by his drone friend. The pair blasted out of the cavern just as the ceiling collapsed, a huge cloud of dust exploding behind them.

'Go, Nuis!' Speck cried as the pair rocketed through the air, riding the turbulent winds. Speck felt his stomach lurch as they spiralled high into the sky, speeding above the jungle and towards the distant *Dawnchaser*.

But just as they were about to catch the ship, Nuis

gave out an alarmed bleep. Speck's eyes widened. He craned his head to look back at the distressed drone. The little bot's lights were fading and its beeps were becoming slurred.

It had only managed to get a little bit of charge back, Speck realised fearfully. Nuis was almost out of battery again.

'You can do it!' Speck urged. 'Just a little further.'

The drone beeped resolutely, but Speck could tell it was fading fast.

They were so close. Speck could see the details on the pirate's angular ship. He could see the fumes wafting from the newly fed boosters and the port hatch almost within grasping distance.

And then they were there! Stretching out an arm, Speck clutched the handle of the port door. He swung his tool belt around his waist and hurriedly set to work gaining access to the ship.

The pirate ship began accelerating forward. Speck let out a cry. Nuis bleeped out in alarm as the drone struggled to keep up with the moving ship. It was going slowly for now, but Speck could imagine Nephora sitting behind the accelerator lever, ready to lean forward on the boosters.

'Hold on, Nuis!' Speck yelled as he jabbed at his console tablet, hacking the hatch's security. 'Nearly there.'

The ship continued to accelerate. Speck's muscles were crying out with pain and he felt his fingers begin to loosen where he clung to the hatch handle for dear life.

His fingers slipped just as his console tablet hacked the port's lock and the hatch flew open. With a final, monumental beep, Nuis caught Speck in its net and flung him through the open hatch. The little drone followed him in, clattering to the floor with a dismal mechanical sigh as the hatch slammed shut behind them.

'We did it,' panted Speck, the realisation only just occurring to him. 'Nuis, we made it!'

He expected to hear Nuis' celebratory bloop echoing in his ear, but after a second there was nothing – only silence. Speck cast his eyes around, looking for his friend.

'Nuis?' he asked.

Then he saw the little drone on the floor, rocking with the motion of the ship. Speck gasped. The drone was dead to the world – completely out of power. Speck could only scoop the bot up and embrace it tightly.

'You saved me, Nuis,' he whispered, hoping that his friend could still hear his words, despite its state of unconsciousness. 'Thank you.'

He looked down at his lost friend for a moment, unsure of what to do. He was certain that if Nuis was awake, the drone would have bleeped furiously at him to not get caught after everything they'd just been through.

The thought shook Speck out of his reverie as he realised that any of the pirates could have heard his noisy entrance. He got to his feet and peered down the corridor. All seemed silent. He took a step forward and grimaced at the sound of his heavy clamper boots on the ship's metal floor.

I'd better lose these, he thought to himself.

Unbuckling his boots, he carefully made his way across to the empty storage shelf that he'd used as his temporary bed and threw them up and out of sight.

He was in the middle of hiding Nuis next to the boots when the patter of footsteps echoed from down the corridor. Speck gasped, hurriedly hauling himself up onto the storage shelf.

The very next moment, Quilch came pacing down the corridor. The little being grasped a laser blaster in one hand. Speck watched as the Quilkin clacked up to the hatch. He looked at the door with a frown and raised a little radio to his beak, twittering a short message.

'What do you mean it's shut?' came Randall's voice over the radio. 'The computer said we had a breach. You'd better check on our captive, just in case.'

Quilch shrugged and, muttering to itself, continued down the corridor. When Speck was certain the Quilkin had gone, he lowered himself back down to the floor.

He followed Quilch as the pirate made his way

to the *Dawnchaser*'s hold. The pirates had turned the storage room into a temporary prison cell and Speck watched as the Quilkin tapped a password into the room's security panel. The door slid open.

Shortly after going in, the pirate emerged again, raising his radio and twittering into it.

'She's still in there?' replied Randall's crackling voice. 'Damn computer must be malfunctioning. The first thing I'm doing after we collect our bounty is replacing this heap of junk.'

The Quilkin chirruped in agreement and started down the hallway. Speck waited until he could no longer hear the being's clacking talons before creeping up to the door and punching in the same code he'd seen the pirate use. The door slid open and Speck entered to find Princess Juni staring morosely out of the hold's single window – a small, circular porthole.

'I told you to leave me alone!' she snapped, but then she saw Speck and her eyes widened in surprise.

'Speck, you're alive!' she cried. 'I was worried about you.'

'You were worried about me?' Speck asked, thinking only about what a precarious situation Juni herself was in.

'Of course, I was. I'm so glad you got off the planet. Just look at it!'

As she spoke, the princess pointed out of the window. Speck looked out to see the ship had broken through the atmosphere of the planet and was now in the vast sea of space. From their vantage point, Speck could witness the entirety of the Lost Planet, but it wasn't a planet at all. Speck watched with stunned fascination as it moved and mutated.

It's uncurling, he realised. As crazy as it seemed, the planet was unrolling and changing from a globe and into a long, thin, snake-like shape. A snake-like shape with a gargantuan, terrifying face.

'A space wyrm!' he gasped, recognising the leviathan immediately. 'The Lost Planet was a space wyrm all along.'

'I think it's just woken up,' Juni said. 'It curls up to sleep. When it slumbers, it acts just like a normal planet. It's unbelievable. Those horrendous winds in that valley must have been it snoring.'

Speck blinked and shook his head.

How can a planet be lost? He realised he'd never got an answer, but now he had. A planet could get lost if it wasn't a planet at all. No wonder the laboratory was built there. Where better to study the powers of a space wyrm?

The Starchild must have woken the wyrm up as he left, Speck realised, and the memory quickly brought him back to his mission.

'Juni,' Speck said, tearing himself away from the phenomenal sight. 'I know where the Starchild is going and I need your help stopping him.'

But Juni was in a world of her own, still staring out the portal at the space wyrm.

'Thrugg is still down there,' she said softly. 'Do you think he'll be okay?'

Speck swallowed.

'I don't know,' he answered truthfully. 'But Thrugg wouldn't have wanted Randall to take you back to Thrakkush. He would have wanted me to stop the Starchild, too.'

Juni slowly nodded, blinking back her tears.

'You're right,' she said. 'But how are we going to take the ship back? There's two of us and three of them. Plus, they all have blasters and we don't have a single weapon between us.'

'I have an idea,' said Speck as confidently as he could muster. 'And I'm about fifty percent certain it'll work.'

At the same moment, Quilch was finishing his rounds of the ship. He trotted back onto the flight deck to find Randall staring in awe through the viewport window as the space wyrm slowly unwound and stretched to its full size.

At the controls, Nephora rolled her eyes.

'Can we go yet? I'm sick of this place.'

'Not yet,' Randall snapped. 'The princess isn't going anywhere.'

Nephora sighed. Her skin had become a consistent shade of blue ever since Randall had taken over as captain.

The other pirates might not understand what that meant, but she knew that she only changed colour when she felt strong emotions. She turned red when she was angry, like she had when she discovered that Captain Oran had lied to her ever since they first met. But now she was blue.

'Look at it!' Randall cried. 'I think it's feeding.' Out in space, the wyrm was circling a star, ripping strands of flame from the celestial orb as if it were sucking at it from a straw.

Nephora turned her head to look, but just as she did her eye caught movement in the reflection of the flight deck window. She frowned. She could have sworn she had just seen the kid.

She swung around in her chair and her mouth fell open.

'Ghost!' she blurted in horror.

Randall and Quilch spun round. Quilch let out a cry of fear, but Randall's face became stony as he saw Speck standing there.

'That's no ghost,' he said. 'Though by all rights, he should be by now. How did you ever manage to get on board my ship, boy?'

'I'm not here to cause trouble,' Speck said hurriedly as Nephora and Quilch both reached for their blasters. 'I need your help.'

Randall's face creased into a smirk. 'You came all this way, unarmed, to ask for our help? Didn't I already tell you, kid? The only person a pirate helps is himself.'

Speck nodded. 'I know, and that's exactly why I came back.'

Randall frowned.

'Go on,' urged Nephora.

'I know where the Starchild is going,' said Speck. 'This time he isn't going to a moon. He's going to a planet with thousands of beings on it. If he isn't stopped, then it could be really bad. I don't know how much gold you're getting for taking the princess to Thrakkush, but I'm sure the Emperor of the entire Galaxy will give you much, much more if you help save an entire planet.'

'Brilliant plan, kid,' Randall said. 'There's only one small flaw. What makes you think that you can stop it?'

'Because I . . . I understand him,' Speck said. 'He was designed to be one thing – a weapon – but that doesn't mean he has to be one. I can talk to him. I can make him change his mind. Please.'

There was silence. Speck looked to the floor, as if any belief he'd had whilst speaking had instantly evaporated. Nephora knew that feeling. She'd endured it enough times herself.

'Nice fantasy, kid,' Randall said. 'But it's time to face reality. Vart, take him to join the princess in the hold.'

'My name is Nephora,' said the Ureyan quietly.

'What?' said Randall, turning to Nephora. His eyes widened as he saw that her skin had flushed a crimson red.

'I told you that Vart is my last name – and I hate it.'

'It hardly matters,' Randall said. 'Just do as I order.'

Nephora's eyes narrowed. She turned her blaster away from Speck and pointed it directly at Randall. His mouth fell open.

'Steady on!' Randall glanced at Quilch. Then, 'Mutiny! Quilch! Blast her!'

Only the Quilkin's blaster also pointed at him.

'You!' the captain said. Quilch merely shrugged, twittering angrily.

'That's right,' Nephora said. 'You said it yourself, Cappin', we go where the gold is. The kid has the better offer.'

Speck smiled, flooded with relief. He looked directly at Randall. 'And what about you? We'll need your help, too.'

Randall's teeth were gritted; his blistering stare blazed with as much fury as the star that was being slowly digested by the colossal wyrm outside.

'I'm the captain,' he spat and his hand darted for the holster on his hip.

Randall froze. His holster was empty.

At that moment, Princess Juni stepped forward. She held Randall's blaster casually in one hand.

'Looks like Quilch isn't the only one good at picking pockets,' she said.

Randall's face contorted.

'You fools!' he muttered, turning to Quilch and Nephora in turn. 'Can't you see that I'm the best captain you'll ever have?'

Nephora ignored him. She turned to Juni instead.

'What should we do with him, Cappin'?' she asked.

Juni shrugged.

'You're asking the wrong person,' the princess said. 'I'm not the one with the plan.'

Juni turned to Speck, as did Nephora and Quilch. They all looked at him expectantly and he felt the pressure of all their eyes weighing on his shoulders.

You can do this, he thought to himself. If you can be a utility droid, a pirate, and a nobody, then you can be a captain.

'Take him to the hold and lock him in,' Speck commanded.

'Aye aye,' said Nephora. Quilch grabbed hold of Randall's shirt and began pushing him out of the flight deck, much to the navigator's ire.

Nephora sat back in the pilot's chair. Out of the viewport the space wyrm was still feasting. The star was smaller now, depleted after the leviathan's hungered frenzy.

'Now,' said Juni. 'We'd better get out of here before it turns that star into a black hole. What's our course, Speck?'

Speck pondered his options. 'The Starchild is going after Giddius Monk,' he thought aloud. 'So he must be heading for the Night Eaters' Headquarters.'

'But that's on Arkanius,' said Juni.

Speck nodded. 'Exactly. Where else to demonstrate

the full potential of his power than on the capital planet of the entire Galaxy? Where better than the emperor's own planet?'

Nephora exhaled slowly as Juni walked across to Randall's old seat.

'Setting a course for Arkanius.' Juni punched in the coordinates to the navigation computer.

'Here goes nothing,' added Nephora.

Speck took one last glance at the majestic space wyrm as it finished feeding. The star was finally extinguished just as the *Dawnchaser* began to rocket forward, jumping into light-speed. The pirates were on course for Arkanius and the wrath of the Starchild. Speck could only hope they wouldn't be too late.

14

The Final Test

Giddius Monk's spaceship, the *Pilgrim*, descended onto the landing platform outside of the Night Eaters' Headquarters. Moments later, Giddius emerged on the embarkment ramp, crimson cloak flapping in the wind. He stopped for a moment at the foot of the ramp and scanned the tall spire that towered before him.

It felt good to be back on Arkanius after such a long time away. What an ordeal it had been! He'd spent months getting to that forsaken laboratory in the middle of nowhere to pick up his new super weapon, only for that fool Bizzabin to prove to be too incompetent. After that, he'd been forced to take Ardulus to the Grand Orbital Library and trick that fool Vargel Pren into letting him experiment on the boy. Then, that other petulant boy, the orphan, had shown up and released Ardulus before he could complete his research.

But it had all worked out in the end, Giddius thought to himself. He couldn't help but smile as he made his way across the landing strip and towards the headquarters of the Guild of Night Eaters.

It was a beautiful morning in Arkanius. The rain was more of a drizzle than a downpour, and the thick layer of clouds that sat in the sky looked beautiful in the early morning light. From his vantage point on the Night Eaters' Headquarters, Giddius could see the expanse of the planet's capital city stretching out in all directions around him and, in the far distance, the intimidating residence of the mysterious Emperor himself.

There lies the true power of the Galaxy, Giddius thought to himself. And soon it will belong all to me.

Monk passed a series of bowing Night Eaters as he entered the headquarters. It had been his father who had designed and built the headquarters, and he couldn't help but think that his forefathers had some of the worst taste in the entire Galaxy.

The first thing I'm going to do when I'm Emperor is tear this place to the ground, he thought bitterly as he took an elevator up to his private quarters on the very top floor. Out with the old, in with the new. He liked that.

Power was all he'd ever wanted. Was it too much to ask for? He enjoyed being the leader of the Night Eaters, of course, but he hated all the responsibilities that came with it. He didn't care for exploring. All the trinkets that adorned his mask were either bought or taken forcibly from his fellow Guild members. No, his particular set of skills was commanding others. It was in his blood.

The elevator finally arrived at the top floor. The door slid open and Giddius stepped out onto the gun-metal grey floors of his quarters. His home was sparse, cold and simple. Just as he liked it. He was just thinking how quiet it seemed to be when a familiar voice echoed in his mind, searing in his ears like a hot iron.

'Hello, father. I've been waiting for you.'

Giddius blinked. Ardulus was floating before him, waiting. His son's eyes were crackling away with their limitless potential. A smile touched Giddius' lips and he reached up to remove his mask.

'Hello, Ardulus,' he said. 'I see you've remembered who you are, at last.'

Ardulus' eyes were blazing brightly as he stared down at his father. The boy's hands clenched and Giddius could see them shaking with poorly contained rage.

Untrained, Giddius thought to himself. We'll need to see to that.

'What you did to me is unforgivable,' whispered the Starchild. 'You will pay for your mistakes.'

Giddius tutted as he shook his head. 'You're entirely too predictable, Ardulus.'

'Stop calling me that!' bellowed the being, and his

eyes burnt brighter than a thousand stars, his body trembling with anger.

He's like a bomb ready to go off, thought Giddius, and I'm the one holding the detonator.

'All I ever wanted was to make you proud of me,' the Starchild said quietly.

'Then do it,' retorted the leader of the Night Eaters. 'Make me proud. If you do one thing for me, then you can prove that you are ready to take your place by my side.'

The Starchild's eyes narrowed. 'You would take me back?'

'Of course.' Giddius smiled as pleasantly as he could muster. 'This has all been a test to see if you have what it takes to be a Monk. And now it is time for the final test.'

'Final test?' Ardulus repeated, intrigued. Like a fish on the end of a line, thought Giddius.

'Do what you do best,' Giddius said. 'Destroy. Destroy this city and you will finally be worthy of my love. Destroy this city and I will welcome you back with open arms.'

'And if I don't?' questioned the Starchild.

'Then I will know I raised a failure,' hissed Giddius.

The Starchild's eyes widened. He snarled and raised his clenched fists to the air.

Giddius took an uneasy step back. Looks like I won't have to order this building's demolition after all, he thought. And he moved one hand to a hidden device on his belt, just as the Starchild let out a destructive scream.

The *Dawnchaser* bucked and rumbled as it flew at light-speed towards Arkanius with Nephora at the controls. Speck sat slumped on the floor of the flight deck. It would take a while to make the journey to the capital planet, even at light-speed. The Lost Planet had been very lost indeed. In the meantime, the pirates had decided to find some food and rest up. It had been a long day.

Arkanius, Speck thought to himself, marvelling still that his adventures had taken him to so many places. He'd read about Arkanius hundreds of times on board the Grand Orbital Library. It was the capital planet of the entire Galaxy and where the Emperor himself lived. Speck had never seen the Emperor, but he'd heard great things. Speck exhaled deeply and he realised just how scared he was. It was down to him to not only stop the Starchild, but save an entire planet.

A polite cough suddenly issued from nearby and Speck looked up to find Juni standing there.

'How are you doing, kid?' she asked. 'I suppose I should stop calling you "kid" now. It's just a force of habit, I suppose.'

'It's okay,' Speck said. 'I definitely feel like a kid compared to you.'

Juni smiled as she slumped against the wall beside him.

'I've been meaning to thank you,' she said. 'For getting my ship back. It's kind of the only home I've known since I left Thrakkush.'

Speck gave the princess a sheepish smile. He'd never been thanked by royalty before.

'How's Nuis doing?' Juni asked, and Speck felt his smile evaporate in an instant. The little drone had been unable to wake up, even after Speck had hooked it up to a power supply. Quilch had offered to try and repair the little bot, but Speck feared the worst.

'Nothing yet,' said Speck, a lump forming in his throat.

'Hey, if Quilch can keep this hunk of junk spaceship running, then I'm sure that he can fix your friend,' Juni comforted.

'It's just scary not having Nuis around,' sighed Speck.

'I know exactly how you feel,' said Juni. 'Thrugg being gone makes me feel so . . . vulnerable.'

Juni fell into silence and Speck examined the princess's face. It was a tough face, softened only by her round nose. Since he'd last seen her, she'd painted a dark strip of face paint across her blistering emerald eyes and tied several golden trinkets into her long snow-white braid.

'It's a tradition on my planet,' she explained, noticing him staring. 'The paint across my eyes symbolises mourning, and each of the trinkets on this braid represent someone close to me who I've lost.'

She moved a hand up to touch the dangling trinkets. 'It's good to be able to wear them again. I had to keep them hidden while I was pretending to be Oran.'

Speck nodded. 'I'm sorry,' he whispered. It was all he could think to say.

'Don't be,' she replied. 'I'll return one day, on my own terms.'

She tried to smile bravely, but Speck could see the fear in her eyes. *She really is just a kid like me*, he thought.

'To think you've seen so much,' Speck said thoughtfully.

'And you haven't?' Juni laughed. 'You're already so much more grown up than when I first met you. Plus, you managed to escape a collapsing alien planet all by yourself. That's pretty impressive if you ask me.'

'Well, I still don't feel like a captain,' he said. 'That's for sure.'

Juni snorted. 'You think I ever did? Look at me. I was a spoilt princess until only a few years ago. My father wouldn't even let me out of the palace for most of my life. I'm the last person you'd ever expect to be leading a band of pirates around the Galaxy.'

'How did you do it?' Speck asked, and Juni bit her lip as she thought.

'I had to pretend,' she explained. 'And after a

while pretending got a little bit easier, and soon it became almost second nature. I think that maybe we're all pretending deep down. You just get better at it with time.'

'But weren't you scared of getting found out?' Speck asked and Juni almost doubled over with laughter.

'Of course I was!' she said. 'I was absolutely terrified, but it takes bravery to be who you want to be. It takes bravery to be responsible for others.'

Speck nodded thoughtfully. He wondered if Juni was right. He couldn't imagine any of the pirates or Night Eaters ever being scared.

'Do you think even the High Librarian gets scared?' Speck wondered.

'Definitely,' replied Juni, as if it was the simplest thing in the world. 'Especially if he had to look after you!'

And they laughed together, filling the flight deck with the merry sound.

At that moment, a familiar blooping noise echoed from down the corridor. Speck's eyes widened when he saw Quilch trotting towards them. He was accompanied by a certain drowsy-looking security drone.

'Nuis!' Speck cried. The drone spotted him immediately and let out an ecstatic bleep.

'Thank the stars you're all right,' Speck cried, hugging the little drone as Quilch twittered like a fussing mother.

'He says that Nuis needs a lot of rest before he's better,' translated Juni. 'So no more anti-grav nets for a while.'

'Thank you, Quilch.' Speck beamed, and the Quilkin saluted with a feathery hand.

Just then, the ship gave a violent shake and Nephora looked round from the pilot's seat.

'Hold on,' she said. 'We're coming out of light-speed in five, four, three, two . . .'

The stars stopped whipping past. The *Dawnchaser* jerked to a halt, and suddenly the planet of Arkanius was there before them: a grey-blue globe covered in swirling cloud.

But even Speck, who had never visited the capital planet before, could tell that something was very wrong. Dotted all over the globe were hundreds of spaceships. They looked small from the distance that the pirates were at, but Speck recognised their shape immediately.

Galactic Imperators, he thought. It was the Emperor's private army.

'That's a lot of Imperator ships,' mumbled Juni, staring out of the viewport window. There must have been over a hundred of the colossal craft hovering in orbit.

'I'd wager that's the whole armada,' said Nephora with a whistle.

'Look!' Juni pointed. 'That huge swirling cloud. That's where they're all headed.'

There was an expansive area of the planet, far

darker than the rest, where angry clouds were swirling around in a spiral as if stirred by a giant spoon.

'I'm taking us in,' said Nephora.

Quilch twittered nervously and Speck didn't need anyone to translate the Quilkin's language. His own stomach was already starting to toss and turn nervously.

'It must be serious,' mumbled Nephora. 'The Imperators are ignoring us completely.'

The pirates shared a look as they followed the traffic. The ship shook and rumbled as it passed into the planet's atmosphere. Nephora expertly guided the craft down through the thick layer of cloud and, as they finally burst through, an expansive city lay stretched out before them.

'Oh no,' Speck said. His mouth was dry. 'We're too late.'

The storm was no natural storm. Not by a long shot. Speck instantly recognised the way the wind, clouds and rain were being sucked towards one central point, a tower that Speck knew as the headquarters of the Guild of Night Eaters. Except the top of the tower had been obliterated and now, sitting atop the remaining spire, was the beginnings of a black hole, slowly growing larger and darker as it fed.

Already, the city immediately around the headquarters was destroyed. Buildings, roads and homes had all been torn from the ground and sucked into the black hole's hungering maw. Speck could see the hulking Imperators swarming around the planet's surface, attempting to evacuate the city.

But there was no way the city could ever be evacuated in time. There were just too many beings and Speck felt his whole world fall away as he realised that it was all his fault.

'What's our plan of attack, Cappin'?' Nephora asked hesitantly, but Speck didn't know. This was worse than he could have ever imagined.

There was a sombre silence, only the howling of the wind outside and the sounds of distant sirens warning the thousands of beings of Arkanius to escape as quickly as they could. Speck couldn't think of anything to say.

Quilch twittered sourly.

'No, Quilch,' said Nephora. 'I don't think there'll be any gold after all. Unless we have a plan.'

Speck swallowed. Not only had he failed his responsibility, but he'd already failed as a captain as well.

'I have a plan,' he said quietly, trying to urge his brain to come up with one on the spot.

'And?' asked Nephora sceptically.

'My plan is – my plan . . .'

He searched his brain. There must have been some way to stop what was happening.

'My plan is to . . .'

And then he stopped talking, because the ship's radio was crackling.

Nephora frowned. 'Odd,' she said. 'We're being hailed. Should I answer it?'

Speck nodded hesitantly and Nephora flicked a switch.

There was crackling, and then a weak voice came through the speakers. A weak but instantly familiar voice.

'Speck?' said the voice. 'Little-bot? Can you hear me?'

Speck's mouth fell open. 'Mother-bot?' he blurted.

The radio crackled with static and then: 'Little-bot! It *is* you!'

Speck's heart was hammering. He could hardly believe it. The other pirates were looking at him with barely disguised confusion, but it didn't matter. He never thought he'd hear his mother-bot's voice ever again.

'Whatever are you doing here, Mother-bot?' he asked. 'You should be on board the Library!'

'I am on board the Library,' crackled the robotic voice on the radio. 'Look above you!'

Nephora pulled back on her levers and the *Dawnchaser* bucked backwards until it was looking directly up.

And there, lowering itself through the dense carpet of clouds, was the only place Speck had ever called home, but in a place he'd never dreamt it could ever exist: the Grand Orbital Library.

★

Speck ran across the Library's vast hangar and embraced his mother and brother in one fell swoop. 'I've missed you both so much!' he cried as he hugged his robot family.

The pirate's ship had docked and the two utility bots had been waiting there to meet them. Vargel Pren was waiting too, and before long the pirates joined the group, huffing and puffing as they struggled to keep up.

Speck had a hundred questions all scrambling to be the first out of his mouth.

'How? How is the Library here? I don't understand.'

The High Librarian chuckled, his weathered wrinkles creasing as he did so. 'The Keepers are the wisest beings in the Galaxy,' he said. 'Naturally, we thought to add a few features to our Library in case of emergencies.'

'So, you flew all the way from Varillis?' Speck asked, stunned.

'The light-speed engines were a little rusty,' admitted the High Librarian. 'But the bots worked overtime to prepare them for the journey.'

'I nearly broke my winch again scrubbing those engines inside and out,' said U-T proudly.

'Then, as we came into orbit, we received a tracking signal telling us that one of our missing security drones was already on the planet,' continued the High Librarian.

'We should have known that it was you,' said M-T. 'Wherever there's trouble, you're never far away.'

Thank the stars for Nuis, Speck thought, as his mother-bot suddenly rushed forward again to hug him tightly.

'Oh, you silly utility bot,' M-T cried. 'How could you be so foolish, sneaking aboard an Imperator ship like that? I was so worried that I had to spend an entire week in the maintenance bay.'

'I'm so sorry, Mother-bot,' Speck said. He could imagine how much his mother-bot would have hated being unable to carry out her duties.

He felt tears threaten to burst forth. He'd been holding them in for so long in front of the pirates, but now he was in the arms of his mother-bot he felt the urge to start crying and never stop.

Keep being brave, Speck, he told himself. Just for a while longer, at least.

'And these are your friends, Speck?' asked the High Librarian, gesturing to the pirates standing at an awkward distance from the reunion.

'Yes,' said Speck. 'They're trying to help me stop the Starchild, but it looks like we're too late.'

Vargel nodded thoughtfully.

'Isn't there any way we can stop the black hole?' Juni asked, but the High Librarian only shook his head.

'I fear not,' he said. 'Only space wyrms have the power to control black holes.'

Speck's eyes widened. He recalled something that Giddius had mentioned to him once as they were both observing the black hole being created back on Calestine.

'The Starchild can close it!' he suddenly cried out loud, much to the High Librarian's surprise. 'Giddius Monk told me as much. The Starchild is filled with the power of a space wyrm. He created the black hole so he can close it again too!'

'Theoretically, yes,' said Vargel, nodding his approval.

'If I can get close enough to the Starchild, I think I can convince him to stop what he's doing,' said Speck, and M-T gave out a mournful wail at the suggestion.

'Nephora,' Speck said, turning to the Ureyan pilot. 'Do you think the *Dawnchaser* could get next to the black hole without being pulled in?'

Nephora bit her lip and her skin flushed orange as she considered the proposal.

'Not for very long,' she said. 'The engines aren't powerful enough.'

Speck frowned.

'Why not utilise the Library?' suggested Vargel Pren. 'It has some of the most powerful engines in the Galaxy.'

'It does?' Speck asked. He had never known that. 'But, High Librarian, if the Library got sucked in, you'd lose all of the research the Keepers have ever done. That's thousands of years of history.'

The ancient Keeper simply smiled. 'The day we value the past over the future is the day that all hope truly is lost,' he said. 'Besides Speck, you're forgetting one vital piece of information.'

Speck gave the High Librarian a questioning look.

'I strongly believe that you're capable of succeeding.'

'Succeeding in what?' M-T cried, still alarmed by Speck's proposal to get closer to the black hole. She wheeled up to her child and clasped hold of him.

'You can't put yourself in danger again, little-bot,' she cried. 'I won't allow it. I've only just got you back!'

'I have to do this,' Speck replied. 'No, I *want* to. I know I can help!' he added with resolve.

Something in his eyes made M-T soften and she slowly nodded, giving him one more tight hug.

'So, what's the plan?' Juni asked.

Speck turned to the expectant pirates. 'It involves all of you,' he said. 'Even the utility bots. We're going to need everyone's help if we're going to stop that black hole from destroying this planet.'

15

Into the Storm

The pieces were in position. Speck stood in one of the many service ducts of the Grand Orbital Library.

In front of him was a utility hatch, which opened out onto the exterior of the ship. A crowd of utility bots were all gathered around him, headed by U-T. They watched as he pulled on his clamper boots and tested that they still worked.

'Okay,' he said after he was confident that the magnets were still functional. 'Is everyone ready?'

'Ready,' said U-T, and he looked over the crowd of amassed bots. 'Winches to Speck-bot, everyone!' he ordered. As one, the bots opened their many chassis and began unwinding their winches, passing the hooks and wires forward to Speck who clipped them all onto his belt.

'Don't forget this hook too, little-bot,' murmured a voice from behind Speck. He turned to find his mother-bot there, offering him the hook of her winch.

'Mother-bot, are you sure?' he asked. 'It could be dangerous.'

'You think that I'm too old and my mechanics will fail, do you?' questioned M-T, nudging him with the hook. 'I'm as strong as the day I was made, and if you think for one second that I'm letting you go out there without my winch stopping you from being sucked into that black hole, then you've got another think coming.'

Speck hugged his mother-bot before taking her hook and clipping it to his belt.

'Everyone ready?' he called out.

A chorus of agreement flooded the area and Speck nodded. Grasping the handle of the utility hatch, he threw the door wide open.

Immediately the wind blasted into the service duct. Speck was bombarded by a flurry of rain and he nearly lost his footing. He might have fallen if it weren't for the crowd of utility bots that had clamped themselves down. As the wind tugged at him, he felt the many ropes attached to his belt going taut with the strain of keeping him anchored down.

'Give me a little slack,' he called, and the ropes began to loosen. He stepped forward so that he was standing on the brink of the hatch. The Night Eaters' Headquarters were before him, the black hole growing stronger by the second.

I hope to the stars this works, thought Speck.

The Grand Orbital Library was slowly drawing

closer to the epicentre of the storm. Its boosters were facing in the opposite direction, roaring loudly as they did their best to keep the ginormous spaceship from being sucked into the growing vacuum.

'Look out!' came a sudden cry from the bots, snapping Speck from his thoughts. He looked up to see a huge chunk of rubble, plucked clean from the city by the storm, flying straight towards the Library. Speck's eyes went wide. He reached for his radio transmitter.

'Juni!' he cried, but suddenly a laser tore through the storm, lighting the sky and hitting the debris. The rubble was instantly shattered into a thousand pieces that rained uselessly against the Library's hull.

'We saw it,' said Juni's voice over the radio as the *Dawnchaser* zoomed past. 'Let us deal with the rubble. You focus on getting to that tower.'

Speck nodded and turned his attention back to the storm's centre. He could see the pitch blackness of the hole as it greedily gulped in the rain like it was dying of thirst. The Starchild was there, floating beneath his creation. Ardulus' head was cast back and his mouth was open in a perpetual scream. Another figure was floating next to the Starchild, but amidst the driving rain Speck couldn't make out who it was, only that they were surrounded by a blue glowing sphere. Who would the Starchild allow to be so close? he wondered.

'Speck,' said a voice over the radio. It was the High

Librarian. 'This is as close as we can get without being sucked in.'

Speck looked out. The distance to the top of the tower was still a long way off.

'Here goes nothing,' he muttered.

'Do be careful, little-bot,' said M-T's voice over the radio.

Speck took a deep breath – and jumped.

In a second, he was snatched up by the gravitational pull of the black hole. He felt his body being whisked towards the remnants of the headquarters. The rain and howling wind battered him as he half fell and half flew through the air and then – oomph!

The wires latched to his belt went taut and he felt the air being driven from his lungs. He was suspended in mid-air, caught in a tug of war between the robots clamped to the Library and the powerful hunger of the black hole. Wiping moisture from his eyes, he looked down to see the floor of the headquarters only a few inches away. If he turned his magnets on, he might be able to clamp down. His sinews ached as he stretched but soon he could feel the magnets pulling him closer to the metal ground. Finally, they clamped down to the floor with a satisfying clang.

I made it, Speck thought with relief.

'You!' came an angered voice from out of the driving rain and Speck looked up with surprise.

It wasn't the Starchild's voice that had spoken, but it was a very familiar voice all the same. The voice had come from the figure hidden within the blue sphere.

'How dare you, boy?' cried Giddius Monk. 'Your part in this tale was over a long time ago.'

'Giddius?' Speck yelled over the howling wind. He was confused. How was the Guild leader here, standing so casually next to the black hole without being sucked in?

'We have to stop the Starchild,' Speck screamed over the roaring wind. 'Otherwise the whole planet will be destroyed!'

But a greedy grin had stolen over Giddius' face. 'You think I don't know that?'

'But . . .' Speck spluttered, taken aback. 'I thought you wanted to stop the Starchild?'

Giddius shook his head. 'The Starchild escaping was never meant to happen, that is true enough, but after you let him loose, I got to see a free demonstration of his true potential. Where better to observe his planet-destroying power than on an outlaw moon that no being will ever care about?'

Speck thought back to Calestine and how he had approached the Guild leader in disguise. He recalled how enthralled Giddius had been with the power of the Starchild that day. The Guild leader hadn't even seemed scared of the black hole at all. In fact, he had seemed almost pleased with it. Now Speck realised, he had been.

'I knew that once the Starchild escaped, he would

eventually find me again,' continued Giddius. 'It was destiny.'

'Because he's your son,' said Speck, and this time it was Giddius' turn to look surprised.

'Why, you have been busy, haven't you?' Giddius grinned. 'You are almost correct. He was my son, but no longer. Now he is the Starchild – the ultimate super weapon.'

'But the Guild of Night Eaters are supposed to be a force of good in the Galaxy,' cried Speck, feeling his voice get whipped away by the furious winds.

Giddius laughed, throwing his head back and cackling into the storm just as a bolt of lightning crackled overhead and was swallowed within the black hole.

'There will be peace,' snarled Giddius, 'when I am made Emperor. No being will ever dare attempt to stand against my will. There will be no fighting or war because no one will dare stand against the might of Giddius Monk!'

Speck felt his hopes deflating. He looked away from the crazed Giddius and up to the Starchild himself, floating just beneath his destructive creation.

'Speck,' crackled the High Librarian's voice over his earpiece. 'We cannot hold on for much longer. The engines are growing too hot. You must act quickly.'

Speck lowered his head and took an agonising step towards the Starchild.

'Not so quick, boy,' growled Giddius, and when Speck looked up, he saw that the Guild leader had a laser blaster in his hand. Monk's free hand went to a set of controls beneath his cloak and the Night Eater began floating effortlessly across to where Speck struggled to stay bolted down.

'Another reason that I should thank you,' he said, gesturing to the blue field around his body. 'It's an anti-grav net generated by my own suit. Clever, don't you think? I got the idea after seeing you fall from the roof of the hangar that night.'

Speck gritted his teeth. He didn't care about the anti-grav suit. His eyes were focussed on the laser blaster pointed directly at him.

'You won't shoot me,' Speck said, hoping he sounded more confident than he felt.

'You're right,' Giddius agreed. 'I'm not evil. I could never bring myself to shoot a defenceless child.' Giddius redirected the blaster until it was pointing behind Speck's back and pulled the trigger. A laser shot fired out in a blinding flash and Speck felt one of the wires attached to his belt suddenly go slack.

'But those winches just aren't secure enough, don't you think?'

Speck gasped. Giddius was shooting the utility bots' wires! Already over his radio he could hear the frantic chatter of fearful droids.

'Speck! Oh, my dear little-bot!' M-T's voice cried over his radio. 'What are we to do?'

Speck craned his neck to look back at the Library. The droids had all repositioned and were now outside, magnetically attached to the Library's hull. As Speck watched, Giddius shot again and again, his laser biting through more wires each time. Speck felt the strain increase on the wires that remained, and on the ship, the droids that were still attached to him cried out as they struggled to stay clamped down.

'I've been cut off!' cried U-T over the radio. 'I'm sorry brother-bot. M-T still has you though.'

'I won't let you go, little-bot,' said M-T and Speck heard the fear even in her mechanical voice.

Speck felt tears bubbling in his eyes. He could feel the black hole starting to win the tug of war. The remaining wires were creaking with the strain, and he was too far away from the Starchild to even be heard by the creature over the deafening storm.

'Looks like the end of the line, boy,' cackled Giddius triumphantly.

But then, as if from nowhere, a laser came flashing through the storm and struck the top of the Night Eaters' Headquarters with a sizzling explosion. The whole building shook violently and with a cry Giddius was knocked to one side. He fumbled his laser blaster and Speck watched as it fell out of the anti-grav net and was immediately snatched up by the black hole.

'No!' Giddius cried, looking towards the black hole with dismay.

Speck could hardly believe his luck. Craning his neck, he peered round to see where the mysterious laser blast had come from. Then he saw, lowering itself down through the thick clouds, the immense shape of one of the Imperators' ships.

Speck's earpiece suddenly crackled and a familiar, gruff little voice spoke over it.

'Friend Speck in need of help,' said the voice, and Speck recognised it immediately.

'Yabba!' he said. 'Just in time!'

'Gumu tribe will give laser cover to friend Speck, no problem,' said the little Gutterling from his craft.

I hope that'll be enough, thought Speck. The wires attached to his belt were still holding, just.

Speck watched as Giddius floated back to where the Starchild was letting loose his perpetual scream. The Guild leader looked up to his son with fury in his eyes.

'Ardulus!' he snapped. 'Do something! That Imperator ship's lasers are too powerful to be sucked into the black hole!'

The Starchild opened his blazing eyes, blinking several times as if waking from a deep dream. He closed his mouth, and as he did, the black hole weakened slightly.

'Help is on the way,' murmured the Starchild.

'What help?' his father questioned, but the Starchild only pointed to where the clouds had been sucked clear from the sky. In their place was a window to outer space, through which the stars were clearly visible.

'I had predicted that we might need some help,'

said the Starchild. 'So I called out to one who will aid us.'

Speck sheltered his eyes from the barrage of rain and squinted. There, amongst the stars, was a shape that was getting closer. It was only small but as it moved it grew larger and larger until it filled the sky – a long, snake-like creature.

'Oh no,' Speck gasped. 'The space wyrm . . .'

'Did he just say "space wyrm"?' Juni demanded from the navigator's chair of the *Dawnchaser*, having heard Speck over the radio.

'Sounded like it,' said Nephora, her face darkly focussed as she steered the ship through the storm.

'That is not good.'

Quilch twittered nervously as he pulled the trigger on the ship's cannons, obliterating another chunk of flying debris that was on a collision course with the Grand Orbital Library.

An alarm sounded on the ship's console, flashing with a red warning. Nephora glanced down at it anxiously and Juni jabbed at the ship's radio.

'High Librarian Pren, this is Juni. The ship's computer is telling me that the black hole has grown too strong for us to withstand. We have to get further away or we'll get sucked in.'

The radio crackled and the High Librarian's voice sounded back through it.

'I understand,' said Vargel Pren. 'It's time for your crew to get clear. There's no point in putting yourselves in more danger than necessary.'

'But what about the Library?' Juni asked fearfully.

'We'll go on for as long as we can manage,' responded the High Librarian. 'We have the utility bots still. They'll patch up any holes as fast as they can.'

'Okay,' said Juni. 'Good luck.' She flicked the radio transmitter off and nodded at Nephora to bring the ship back from the hungering black hole.

'Now what?' asked the despondent Ureyan as the ship glided away from the storm. Juni looked down at the city as they went, watching hundreds of Imperators helping to evacuate the citizens of Arkanius as quickly as possible. But she knew in her heart that they couldn't all be evacuated in time. And this was only one city. What would happen when the whole planet was destroyed?

Looking up through the viewport window, she saw the hole that had formed in the clouds of Arkanius. Speck had been right. There, high above the planet's surface, was the distant form of the space wyrm, growing ever larger by the second. When it reached the planet, it wouldn't matter if the black hole had finished forming or not. A wyrm that size could smash a planet in two with ease.

Juni clicked the radio transmitter.

'Any available craft follow me,' she ordered over

an open frequency. 'We have to try and stop that space wyrm from getting to this planet.'

'What?' Nephora cried. 'Have you lost your mind?'

'We can't just sit here and do nothing,' said Juni, reaching for the radio again. 'I repeat, all available craft, come with us to intercept that space wyrm.'

There was a crackle of static and then:

'Yabba and Gumu tribe will help. Rest of Gutterling tribes help also. Lead the way, friend of friend of Gumu tribe!'

Juni nodded to Nephora and the Ureyan shrugged.

'I hope to the stars you know what you're doing,' the Ureyan said before accelerating up towards space and the approaching wyrm.

16

The Curse of the Starchild

Speck felt his heart fall as he watched the Imperator ships retreating towards space to face the approaching space wyrm, but Giddius only laughed.

'Brilliant, Ardulus. I couldn't have planned it better myself. You truly are my son. Nothing can stop us now.'

'Yes, father,' said the Starchild, and he closed his eyes, ready to resume his tantrum.

'Wait!' Speck cried, as loud as he could muster. He felt his throat burning with the strain. The Starchild's blazing eyes flickered open and they found Speck amidst the storm.

'You!' said the Starchild, startled. 'You escaped the laboratory.' As usual, his voice didn't come from his mouth. Instead, it was woven into the very fabric of the storm itself, burning into Speck's mind.

'You have to stop this!' Speck cried out.

'I cannot stop now,' replied the Starchild sombrely.

'I must fulfil my purpose.'

'You're too late, boy,' snorted Giddius. 'Don't you see that yet?'

'It's never too late!' Speck shouted, taking another lumbering step closer.

The Starchild watched Speck, blazing eyes hesitating momentarily, but then he shook his head. 'I'm afraid it is,' he said. 'It is my power as it is my curse.'

'It's not a curse,' Speck called back, and it felt like the driving rain and blustering wind were dying down slightly. Suddenly, his hoarse voice was carrying a little better on the wind.

'I understand how you feel, Ardulus,' Speck continued. 'You tricked me when we first met, but I think you still meant what you said. You really were lost.'

The Starchild's eyes narrowed.

'I'm not lost,' he said. 'I know exactly who I am. I'm the Starchild.'

'Then why are you doing what he tells you?' Speck asked, jabbing a finger towards Giddius.

'Because I am Ardulus Monk,' said the Starchild quietly.

'Which is it then?' Speck demanded. 'Are you the Starchild or are you Ardulus?' Doubt flittered across the Starchild's face and his hands trembled as he glanced between Speck and Giddius.

'Stop confusing him,' snarled Giddius, turning to

the Starchild. 'You are my son. Your name doesn't matter. All that matters is that you destroy this planet when I tell you to.'

The Starchild glanced again between Speck and Giddius, his flaming eyes burning with anguish.

'I don't know!' he cried out.

And then he threw his head back and roared with hot anger. Speck saw Giddius' eyes widen in shock as a tsunami of energy burst forth from the Starchild's shaking body, heading straight for them both.

The closer they got to the space wyrm, the more Juni realised how futile the pirates' mission was. The space wyrm was the size of a planet, and even the Imperator's vast ships were smaller than fleas compared to the immense creature. She could only watch with despair as the Imperator craft lined up alongside the *Dawnchaser* and let loose a barrage of laser fire to absolutely no effect. The space wyrm floated past the armada, continuing on towards Arkanius and ignoring them completely.

'Its skin is too thick,' said Juni. 'It doesn't even realise we're attacking it.'

'If only we could get under its skin,' mused Nephora. 'I'm sure then it wouldn't be so happy about our lasers.'

Juni's eyes widened.

'That's it!' she said. 'The windy valley! That

crevice was deep. I bet if we flew into it, we could get under the skin and make ourselves noticed.'

Quilch twittered in disdain.

'Quilch is right,' said Nephora. 'We don't even know how to find that valley again. The wyrm is the size of an entire planet, remember?'

'Yes, but if we had the coordinates . . .' Juni said, straining her memory. There was something she was missing. Speck had mentioned something during his retelling of his escape from the Lost Planet, but what was it he'd said?

A Gutterling! That was right. He had told her that a Gutterling lived in a secret laboratory down on the wyrm's body!

She clicked her radio on and leaned towards the microphone.

'Yabba of the Gumu tribe, can you hear me?'

'Yes, Yabba can hear,' came a gruff little voice over the radio.

'Yabba, do you know of a Gutterling who lives on that space wyrm?' she asked. 'I think her name is Om . . . or Nom, or something.'

'Nom of Ogga tribe?' came the Gutterling's chirpy response.

'Yes, that's the one!' Juni cried. 'Are you able to hail Nom on the radio?'

'Why, yes,' said Yabba thoughtfully. 'She is in a top-secret location only to be hailed for emergency, but Yabba would say this is emergency, no?'

'Of course it is!' cried an exasperated Juni.

'Okay then, Yabba just be a moment.'

There was a series of mutterings as the Gutterling went to work and Juni could only sit anxiously as she watched the space wyrm drawing closer to the planet. Finally, there was a burst of static on the radio.

'Hello? This is Nom of Ogga tribe,' said a frail voice over the radio.

'Greetings, Nom of Ogga tribe,' Yabba said in a highly pleased voice. 'This is Yabba of Gumu tribe. How does Nom do today?'

'Nom is very well, thank you,' Nom replied. 'Nom has just made some yum-yum mushroom soup. It is very tasty. How goes the science-making?'

'It goes very well, thank you,' replied Yabba. 'Why, just other day Yabba was –'

'We don't have time for this!' cried a frantic Juni. She couldn't believe it. 'Nom, we require the coordinates of your laboratory. Please, it's an emergency.'

'Emergency?' Nom said. 'Well, why did friends not say?'

Juni shook her head and as the coordinates came through she caught Nephora smirking in the corner of her eye.

'Gutterlings . . .'

'All right,' said Juni. 'Let's do it.'

'Aye aye, Cappin',' Nephora said, leaning forward on the accelerator and bringing the ship down towards the surface of the planet-sized wyrm.

The ship plummeted through the atmosphere and was soon soaring through the thick mists that coated the mysterious wyrm's body. Nephora carefully weaved between the towering trees that spouted from the creature's flank.

'They're the wyrm's hairs,' said Juni thoughtfully, looking out at the trees with dawning realisation.

Suddenly Quilch twittered in excitement, pointing out of the viewport window. Juni followed his feathered finger.

'Yes, Quilch!' she cried, excitedly. 'There's the chasm!'

The windy gulch was right where they had left it, as was the bridge that spanned across it.

'Stay alert on the scanners,' Nephora said. 'We're going in.'

The Ureyan smiled grimly and rolled the ship forward, flicking on the ship's headlights as it was swallowed by the shadows of the chasm.

Juni nodded and took a deep breath. She was about to turn to look at her computer screens when –

Thud!

Something hit the hull of the ship. She looked about with wide eyes.

'What was that?' she asked, but she could tell from the looks of her fellow pirates that neither of them knew either.

Thud! Thud! Thud!

More! Something was slamming into the ship as it descended deeper. The hits sounded weak and distant, as if whatever was hitting into them was only soft – or maybe squishy.

Thud! Thud! Thud! Thud!

More and more and then dark shapes began crawling over the viewport window. Dark writhing shapes with mouths full of sharp teeth.

'Shriekers!' she cried out. 'Those blasted bugs!'

The ship began to buck and weave as Nephora wrestled with the controls.

'They're everywhere!' she snarled, her skin flushing red with rage. 'I can't control the ship! They must be clogging the boosters.'

Juni held on tightly as the ship became unresponsive to Nephora's commands. They began to swerve dangerously to one side and, with a sharp jolt, grazed the side of the chasm. The impact made a horrible crunching sound and Juni was thrown from her seat.

'Hold on!' Nephora cried. Juni felt her stomach fill with butterflies. The ship continued to fall, hitting the sides of the chasm and tumbling down until, with a terrifying bang, it crashed down, coming to a bone-shuddering halt at the bottom of the valley. The craft's headlights finally flickered out as the slimy shriekers continued to pile onto the lifeless craft.

Juni scrambled to her feet, her body aching in a hundred or more different places.

'Let's not do that again in a hurry,' she muttered

as Nephora and Quilch also gathered themselves.

The ship's power was completely out. The lights of the computer consoles had been extinguished.

'Can we get the engines started?' she asked hesitantly, but Nephora shook her head.

'It's the shriekers,' she said. 'They're everywhere.'

Juni sighed deeply and, reaching for her laser blaster, headed towards the back of the flight deck. Quilch twittered aghast as he saw where Juni was going.

'That's right,' Juni said. 'I'm going out there.'

'You can't be serious,' gasped Nephora. 'You won't last a second.'

'Someone's got to try and unclog those engines.'

Juni was about to open the port hatch when Quilch began tweeting in a hysterical tone.

'You can't stop me, Quilch, and that's final!' she said, exasperated, but when she turned, she saw that the Quilkin wasn't looking at her. Instead, he was pointing out of the viewport window.

'You saw a light?' Juni asked, frowning. 'Where?'

Juni peered out of the window but could only see the thriving mass of shrieking bugs trying to gnaw at the outside of the ship.

Quilch must finally have gone space crazy, thought Juni with a sigh, but at that moment she saw it too – a glowing light coming from beyond the frenzied insects. It glimmered through every time there was a break between the bodies of the squirming shriekers.

'What is that?' Juni squinted her eyes.

The light was glowing brighter and brighter. It was a warm light, almost like fire. But what was fire doing down here?

A jet of flame suddenly erupted over the viewport window in a blazing wave of heat. The despicable creatures immediately scattered and fled amid loud shrieks of pain.

The window was clearing. The pirates could see through it and standing there, amidst a cloud of angry shriekers, was a very scarred and beaten-up gladiator from the planet Thrakkush.

Scarred and beaten-up, but very much alive.

'You leave ship alone!' Thrugg bellowed as he ignited his flamethrower once more.

'Thrugg!' Juni cried, hardly able to believe her eyes.

'The shriekers are leaving!' Nephora reported excitedly as more of the bugs scattered. 'The engines are back online.'

'Thrugg's saved us!' Juni cried ecstatically. 'Quick! Get him on board!'

Quilch saluted and joined her as she scrambled toward the port hatch.

Between them, Juni and Quilch hauled the wounded gladiator back onto the ship, pulling him up the embarkment ramp before the shrieking swarm could re-focus its efforts. As the hulking warrior saw Juni, he beamed from ear to ear.

'Juni alive!' Thrugg bellowed and Juni jumped up to embrace the gladiator tightly.

'Of course I'm alive, you big dummy,' said Juni, tears trickling down her cheeks. 'It was you that we were worried about!'

The gladiator burst into tears of joy. 'Juni alive.' He kept repeating it over and over.

'You're hurt,' she said fearfully as she surveyed her former bodyguard's heavily bruised frame.

'Thrugg fall far,' replied the gentle gladiator. 'Thrugg hurt in lots of places, but Thrugg built strong.' Then the gladiator frowned as if just noticing a vital detail for the first time. 'Hey,' he said slowly. 'Juni is not Captain Oran.'

Juni laughed. 'It took you long enough to notice, you big dolt. I thought it was about time I looked like myself again.'

Thrugg nodded. 'Much better than ugly pirate captain,' agreed the lumbering gladiator.

Juni grinned, kissing Thrugg on the cheek.

Suddenly, Juni's radio crackled to life and Nephora's voice came calling from the flight deck.

'Cappin', I hate to interrupt, but you might want to see this.'

'Come on,' Juni said, grasping the gladiator's hand. 'We're in the middle of a mission.'

Juni and Thrugg arrived back at the flight deck. The ship was airborne once more and the headlights switched on. The twin beams were cutting through the swathes of shadow and before them they saw a large cavern carved into the bottom of the chasm. Except it wasn't a cavern at all because there was no rock; the walls were all formed by slick, twitching muscle.

'This is it,' said Juni excitedly. 'We're under the space wyrm's skin. Let's fire some lasers and get out of here before those wretched bugs return.'

'Aye aye, Cappin',' agreed Nephora.

Quilch saluted and, grasping his controls, fired the ship's guns.

A laser shot out from the ship and into the cavern, sizzling and burning as it bit into the space wyrm's muscles. The reaction was immediate as the valley began quaking all around them and the deafening sound of the wyrm roaring in pain reverberated through the ship.

The radio crackled and Yabba's garbled voice sounded through it.

'Yabba cannot believe his eyes,' yelled the Gutterling over the radio. 'Big hulker wyrm is mighty distracted, like it got big itch it trying to scratch. Pirate friends must keep doing whatever it is they are doing!'

Juni grinned.

'It might only buy him a few extra minutes,' she said. 'But let's hope it's enough. Looks like the rest is down to Speck.'

★

A piercing roar reverberated across the surface of the planet and Speck looked up to see the space wyrm squirming in agony. At least it was no longer moving towards the planet – for now.

He shook his head, still trying to make sense of what had happened after Ardulus had screamed. A wave of pure energy had burst forth from the Starchild, and Giddius had cried out as he was thrown back, blasted away through the maelstrom in his anti-grav net before being lost to the swirling clouds. Only Speck's clamper boots had saved him from a similar fate, but even then the blast had winded him. He'd needed to fight back the urge to throw up.

The Starchild remained floating in the same place. His eyes were wide and blazing brighter than Speck had ever seen, but with Giddius gone this might be the best chance he would ever get to reason with him.

'Starchild!' Speck cried. 'Listen to me!' But even though the Starchild had his eyes open, it was obvious he couldn't hear Speck. He had returned to his stupor and Speck's voice was once more lost in the storm.

'Hurry, Speck!' urged the High Librarian in his ear. Speck had never heard Vargel Pren sound so panic-stricken before, and the tone of the wise Keeper's voice made a shiver fall down his spine. 'The engines are overheating. We can't hold our position any longer.'

Speck turned back to the Starchild and, gritting his teeth, took another agonising step towards him.

Now the right foot, he thought. You can do this.

He was getting closer, but the closer he got, the more the gravity wrenched at him. It felt like his whole being was getting sucked into the hole and the light was bleeding all around him. But he had to keep going.

'Starchild!' he roared over the wind, his voice whipping away into the black hole as soon as it left his lips. 'Starchild!' he cried out, throat stinging with exertion.

The being known as the Starchild twitched slightly.

'Please, Starchild. You must snap out of it!'

The Starchild's eyes dimmed slightly. His head tilted a little towards the approaching figure.

'Why do you continue to try when you know it is futile?' the being asked him calmly.

'Because I understand what you're going through,' Speck said. He felt like his whole body was being plucked clean from his boots. 'You can't let anyone else tell you what you are.'

The Starchild looked down at Speck.

'You're only saying these words to save the lives of your friends,' muttered the Starchild.

'That's part of it,' Speck agreed. 'But they're not the only ones who can be saved. You can too, Ardulus.'

The Starchild flinched slightly.

'You can be the son of Giddius, or you can be the Starchild, but there's another choice,' Speck pressed. 'You can be something else entirely.'

Speck's words seemed to hang in the air, despite all else being sucked into the vacuum of the black hole. He could feel his feet slipping out of his clamper boots. He could hear the fraying of the wires behind his back. He could see, in his mind's eye, the engines of the Grand Orbital Library failing . . .

'Maybe . . .' whispered the Starchild. The being was deep in thought and Speck felt hope rekindle in his heart, just for a moment, but then a voice cut through the wind, laden with insane malice.

'You stupid child!'

Speck spun to see Giddius Monk soaring through the air in his anti-grav net, returning to the top of the Night Eaters' Headquarters. His hair was singed, his eyes were flickering with anger. As he landed on the top of the tower, he reached beneath the folds of his tattered crimson cloak to unsheathe a hidden knife.

'It's time to finish this, once and for all,' he snarled. With a shout of rage, he brought the knife back and swung it through the air, right towards Speck's heart.

Suddenly, a grey blur came hurtling through the air from the direction of the Grand Orbital Library. The blur collided with Giddius, and the Guild leader cried out as he was knocked back by the blow. And then Speck realised what it was – or more precisely – who it was.

'Mother-bot!' he cried.

M-T had unclamped herself from the Grand Orbital Library and, using the black hole's pull, launched herself at the Guild leader. Now she was clinging to Giddius with all her might.

'Get away from my little-bot,' growled M-T as she shook with anger.

'Mother-bot, no!' Speck screamed as he reached out, attempting another staggered step towards the entangled pair. The pain of walking was immense and stars swam dizzyingly before his eyes, but he had to help his mother-bot.

Giddius' look of shock was fleeting 'You're just as much of a fool as the boy is,' he snarled. 'You stupid little utility bot.'

'I may just be a utility bot,' said M-T, quivering with anger. 'But only a utility bot can do this.'

A little port popped open on M-T's chassis and from it sprung forth a single spark of electricity that zapped Giddius in the chest.

Giddius jerked with surprise as the electricity jolted him, but the look of shock was instantly replaced with mocking joy. 'Pathetic!' he said. 'Was that supposed to stop me?'

'No,' replied M-T simply. 'It was only meant to distract you.'

'Distract me?' The Guild leader frowned. His eyes darted down, just in time to see a hand reaching into his anti-grav net. Speck was reaching forward, straining with all his might, and with a final monumental cry he lunged, his finger connecting with the power switch on Giddius' belt.

Giddius' eyes widened with terror as his anti-grav net powered down instantly. The Guild leader's mouth opened to emit a scream, but before he could manage to utter a single syllable, he was swept off his feet. No longer immune to the black hole's gravitational pull, the leader of the Guild of Night Eaters was yanked up into the waiting maw and his shout of rage sang out just as he was swallowed whole, disappearing into the void.

'Speck!' M-T cried urgently. She too was being whipped up towards the black hole, but her winch was still attached to Speck's belt. Speck grunted as her weight was added to the forces dragging him into the unfathomable darkness.

'Hold on, Mother-bot!' Speck yelled. She was caught between Speck and the hole itself, snarled in a deadly tug of war. Speck wrapped his hands around the wire and heaved with all his might.

'Little-bot – my winch is breaking,' said M-T with despair.

Speck shook his head. He refused to believe it.

'No, Mother-bot. I won't let you go,' he said, tears brimming in his eyes.

'You must,' the utility bot sighed. 'I'm so sorry.'

Speck's breath was caught. He looked up to his

mother and the hungering black hole behind her. He turned to see the Starchild. The all-powerful being was staring into the black hole into which his father had just disappeared.

'Starchild! Please! Help us,' Speck begged.

'Your mother,' spoke the Starchild calmly, his voice burning through Speck's mind. 'You love her very much. And she loves you.'

Speck turned back to M-T. The wire holding them together was fraying. It would snap in a matter of seconds.

'My father did not love me,' continued the Starchild.

The wire was held by a single sinew. Speck felt it cutting into his hands as he grasped it tightly, not wanting to ever let go.

'I understand now,' said the Starchild.

The wire snapped. Speck screamed as his mother was swept towards the black hole.

The Starchild clicked his fingers and the hole shrank instantaneously, vanishing into nothingness.

The world was instantly flung into chaos. It was as if the very fabric of space was an elastic band that had been stretched and stretched and suddenly released. Speck felt his whole body go flying backwards. Through the corner of his eye, he saw his mother being flung back onto the roof of the Night Eaters' Headquarters. Across the city, pieces of rubble and debris were swirling in a maelstrom. There was a humungous, deafening din as all of this happened at once, but then, just as suddenly, the rumbling roar faded to nothing and a haunting silence descended upon the capital city.

Speck scrambled to his feet and looked across frantically to see M-T groaning as she pulled herself up onto her wheels.

With a grin, Speck raced across to M-T, embracing her as tightly as he possibly could, despite her metal angles being uncomfortable to hug at the best of times.

'Mother-bot, are you all right?' he asked.

'Of course I am, little-bot,' sighed his mother. 'As long as you are.'

And M-T hugged him back, just as tightly.

He couldn't believe it. The black hole was gone. He breathed a sigh of relief. The black hole was gone and the planet was still there.

They had succeeded.

17

Speck of the Stars

The world seems so quiet now that the storm is over, Speck thought, and he finally felt his pounding heart slow a little as he embraced his mother-bot.

The black hole had been stopped. The light of the nearest star was pouring through the hole left in the clouds. Speck could hear the distant sirens in the city and the gentle patter of rainfall.

'Thank you for showing me what I should have seen all along,' said a voice that Speck had never heard before. Speck span, perplexed, and his eyes widened. It was the Starchild who was speaking, but he was using his mouth. He was using the voice of Ardulus Monk.

'I let anger and fear drive me,' said the all-powerful being quietly. 'I was wrong to do so.'

Speck looked up at the creature floating above him. For once he believed the being's look of misery was no trick.

'I'm sorry about your father,' Speck said quietly and the Starchild looked to the ground. His blazing eyes seemed to have died down somewhat since the black hole had been extinguished.

'I am the one who should be sorry,' said the Starchild. 'I was so angry and afraid that I didn't even think about how selfish I was being. Thank you for reminding me how precious life can be. I had almost forgotten what it was to be human.'

Speck smiled softly.

'I will call off the space wyrm, and then I will depart,' said the Starchild, looking out at the many Imperator ships that were already closing in on the scene of the recent storm. 'I will make sure my power never falls into the wrong hands again.'

'Where will you go?' Speck asked.

'I think I may travel the stars,' said the Starchild thoughtfully. 'I will witness the sights that exist in the deepest corners of the Galaxy. I will find a new purpose. A purpose of my own creation.'

Speck nodded and, reaching up, grasped the Starchild's hand briefly.

'Thank you, Ardulus,' he said. The Starchild nodded and a soft smile touched his lips.

'Thank you, Speck,' he said. 'And perhaps, if you ever wish it, I can help you, too.'

'Help me?' Speck asked.

'Yes. The void whispers to me. It is difficult to explain, but the stars are always watching and they hold infinite wisdom. I'm sure the void even knows where you came from, Speck. Who you truly are.'

Speck's mouth gaped open.

'If you ever wish to discover your true place in the Galaxy, then seek me out. I will be waiting on the third moon of Zor. But for now, I bid you farewell, Speck.'

And with that, the being known as the Starchild clicked his fingers and disappeared into thin air, leaving only the boy, his mother-bot, and the whistling wind.

The rest of that day felt like a dream. The Galactic Imperators arrived shortly after the Starchild's departure. The stout creatures filed out from their ships, laser rifles at the ready and prepared for action.

While the Imperators made sure that the area was safe, Nephora brought the *Dawnchaser* down to dock. All the pirates – and a drowsy-looking Nuis – piled out, hugging Speck. They were all eager to hear what had happened on the planet's surface while they had been battling the formidable space wyrm. Speck was over the moon to see Thrugg again and the gladiator almost squashed all the breath out of Speck as he embraced the boy tightly.

'Speck save the day!' The gentle giant laughed, and Speck laughed with him.

The top of the Night Eaters' Headquarters soon

became crowded and Speck was at once overjoyed and a little daunted to see so many familiar faces. At one point, he even thought he saw the face of Captain Oran within the milling crowd and had to quickly remind himself that the captain no longer existed – at least under that particular guise.

It's been a long few days, he thought to himself.

Speck, M-T, and the pirates were soon informed that they had been summoned to the palace of the Emperor himself. Speck had never met an Emperor before and so he nervously boarded the pirate's ship, along with M-T, to make the short journey across to the grand palace.

'Quilch, you'd better go check on our captive,' said Juni as the ship sped over the city. 'I nearly forgot about Randall amidst all the chaos. I imagine he might be a little shaken after all that carnage with the space wyrm.'

The Quilkin gave an affirmative tweet before shuffling out of his chair and trotting down the corridor.

'I can't wait to see Randall's face when he sees that Thrugg is all right,' Nephora said.

'Me neither.' Juni winked. 'Or when we tell him we managed to stop the Starchild.'

Despite Juni's excitement Speck gave out a soft sigh.

'What's wrong, little-bot?' asked M-T, looking up at her son enquiringly.

'Oh, it's something the Starchild said,' Speck replied. 'He told me to come find him if I want to know who my parents are – my birth parents,' he added with a guilty glance down at M-T.

'Will friend Speck go?' Thrugg asked.

Speck frowned and as he did, M-T tenderly squeezed his hand in her little claw.

'If the time comes when you want to find out then I'll take you myself,' she said.

Speck smiled and squeezed his mother-bot's claw back.

At that moment Quilch came darting back onto the flight deck, twittering in alarm. Juni's head snapped to the panic-stricken Quilkin as the being twittered in its language.

'Gone?' she replied to the little being's urgent tweets. 'What do you mean gone?'

Everyone hurried to follow Quilch to the ship's hold, but the little being was right. It was empty. Randall had disappeared.

Juni mumbled as she paced the flight deck. 'After the power went out the locks on the doors must have failed,' she said. 'And I can't find my phantom suit either.' She mouthed a silent scream. 'What a fool! I completely forgot I left it lying around. He must have slipped out while we were docked at the Night Eaters' Headquarters.'

Speck's eyes widened as he realised that perhaps he had seen Captain Oran earlier, after all.

'Well, there's not much we can do about it right now,' said Juni. 'I'll send a message to the Imperators to keep an eye out, but he's smart enough to program that suit to look like anybody in the entire Galaxy.'

Quilch twittered darkly.

'Let's just hope he's learnt his lesson,' said Juni as they all headed back to the flight deck.

The Grand Orbital Library had returned to space after the black hole had been stopped, but both U-T and Vargel Pren were awaiting the pirates' arrival outside the Emperor's intimidating palace.

'You did it brother-bot,' said U-T as Speck embraced him. 'And about time too. Life was getting so boring without you there to keep getting me in trouble.'

Speck grinned. 'I'm sorry I broke your winch again,' he said. 'Though I think this time it might be worth all the kitchen duty.'

U-T looked up at Speck, shock clearly visible in his ocular system. 'I hadn't thought about that,' he moaned despairingly.

'Well done, Speck,' said the High Librarian as Speck turned to hug Vargel. 'You made all of us Keepers very proud today. We're very lucky to have you amongst our number.'

'Thank you, High Librarian,' replied Speck. 'It's funny, but I don't think any of this would have happened if I had never been made Giddius' assistant in the first place.'

At this the Keeper chuckled softly.

'That may have been a calculated move on my part,' he said. 'I always had my suspicions about Giddius – ever since he came to me requesting to use our laboratories – and I had a feeling that you had a part to play in what was about to transpire. I'm glad to report that my inkling was well-founded.'

Speck frowned. 'You mean you knew this was going to happen?'

'Certainly not,' confessed Pren. 'But I knew your natural curiosity would come through, and that your spirit would see you through to the end. See, that is where Giddius went wrong. He failed to see something rather important indeed.'

'What was that?' asked Speck.

'That even the best laid plans can be derailed by the tiniest speck,' Pren said.

Speck grinned.

'Now,' continued the High Librarian. 'Let us go inside. It is terribly bad manners to keep an Emperor waiting.'

Quilch twittered excitedly and Juni gave the Quilkin a sour glance. 'Trust you to still be thinking about gold,' she said, shaking her head.

The friends headed into the palace and were shown through the regal halls by a burly Imperator. It wasn't long before they were all standing in the Emperor's audience chamber.

At the front of the cavernous room was an empty

throne draped in red satin. Behind the elegant chair was a door, and above the door was a large banner emblazoned with the sigil of the Emperor. Speck turned to the High Librarian, foot tapping nervously.

'Is the Emperor nice?' he asked in a whisper.

'Nobody knows,' replied the ancient Keeper. 'He is notoriously secretive. Even I have never seen the Emperor. I must admit, I'm rather curious myself.'

Speck was about to ask more, but just then an Imperator, even larger than the guards, stepped forward.

'Announcing His Excellency,' spoke the Imperator. 'The champion of peace throughout the Galaxy – Emperor Vizil Battabeng the fourth!'

A respectful hush fell over the gathered crowd. The door behind the throne opened and the Emperor emerged.

Thrugg gasped. M-T clucked. Juni stifled a giggle and Speck's eyes went wide.

The Emperor strolled out, observing those who awaited his arrival. He wore a resplendent blue cloak and held a cane beneath one arm. A monocle rested in one of his beady eyes and his ears were pierced with the most precious gemstones imaginable. But despite all of the finery, the Emperor's fur was still covered in little patches of grease, just like the rest of his race.

'The Emperor is a Gutterling,' Speck gasped and Vargel Pren chuckled at his surprise.

'I had my suspicions,' said the Keeper. 'What other creature could keep the Galaxy united in peace for so long other than a humble Gutterling?'

The Emperor daintily made his way forward and Speck realised that he'd been so taken aback by the appearance of the supreme ruler, that he hadn't even noticed that Yabba had entered at the same time. The Gumu scientist was wearing his best tunic, with only several oil stains on it, and he'd made an effort to scrub some of the grime out his fur. He looked extremely pleased with himself. The scruffy scientist waved to Speck cheerfully as the Emperor came to a halt in front of the band of adventurers.

'This is the one who stopped the black hole?' asked the Emperor as he eyed Speck through his monocle.

'Yes, Emperor Battabeng of all tribes,' replied Yabba with a bow. 'This is Speck. Friend to Gumu tribe. Friend Speck stopped the Starchild and saved the planet.'

'I see,' said the Emperor, and he turned his attention back to the boy who stood before him. 'Battabeng thinks that Speck is no longer friend to just the Gumu tribe. No, Speck is friend to all. What is the tribe of friend Speck? Emperor Battabeng must thank his new friend properly.'

'My tribe?' Speck asked, shuffling his feet. 'I don't have a tribe – Your Excellency. I'm an orphan you see, raised by robots and the Keepers.'

'Hmm.' The Emperor thoughtfully scratched the

tip of his pointed nose with a yellowed claw. 'No tribe? I think you mistaken, friend Speck. Emperor Battabeng think you do have tribe. The whole Galaxy your tribe now. You make it so with brave actions.' As he spoke, the Emperor's eyes lit up as if he'd thought of something that pleased him greatly. 'Yes, your tribe be entire hulking Universe. So we shall know new friend as Speck of the Stars!'

Speck bowed deeply, feeling his face flushing. In the corner of his eyes he could see M-T watching him, hardly able to keep still, bursting as she was with the upmost pride for her little-bot.

'Hear Battabeng!' cried the Emperor, turning to those gathered around them. 'Emperor pronounces Speck of the Stars not only chimi choro yoko – friend to all Gutterlings, but chimi choro oro – friend to all!'

'Chimi choro oro!' cried the assembled Imperators in a booming chorus.

'Now, friend Speck,' continued the Emperor, turning back to the boy with a warm smile. 'Battabeng believes that Speck should be rewarded for his courage.'

Speck's mouth went dry. He hadn't thought to be rewarded for what he had done. He had never expected to even be thanked for stopping the Starchild. It was his fault in the first place and he told the Emperor as much.

'Tish tosh,' tutted the Emperor. 'Mistakes happen all time. Beings all across Galaxy make mistakes, but not all beings work so hard to make mistakes right again. That why Speck is friend to all.'

'Oh,' said Speck, feeling relieved.

The Emperor smiled. 'Battabeng has considered reward for new friend and decided that Guild of Night Eaters needs new leader. Last one go mysteriously missing during storm, no? Emperor Battabeng think that friend Speck would make grand leader of Night Eaters.'

Speck covered his mouth with his hand. To be a member of the Night Eaters was always his dream. No matter how evil Giddius had turned out to be, the explorers were still his idols.

But to be the leader of the entire Guild . . . He could hardly believe it! For a moment he could see himself donned in a crimson cloak and mask, heading up an exploration in some uncharted area of deep space: a hero.

But there was something wrong with that image, something very wrong.

'I can't accept that reward,' Speck said, and even Vargel Pren looked surprised. 'I would love to be the leader of the Night Eaters,' Speck continued hurriedly. 'But this all happened because somebody was in charge who shouldn't have been. The Guild needs someone who is already an experienced leader, someone who cares for all beings great and small and doesn't care for glory or gold, but cares for what's right.'

Speck turned and looked at Juni. 'Someone like you.'

Juni's mouth dropped open.

'But kid, I don't deserve that,' she said. 'You were the one who saved the day.'

Speck shook his head. 'I don't need to be a Night Eater anymore. Besides, I only just became Speck of the Stars.'

He looked up to the High Librarian, who gave him a knowing wink.

'Your Excellency,' said Speck, turning back to the Emperor. 'I thank you for your kind offer, but I believe that Juni, former princess of Thrakkush, should lead the Night Eaters.'

'Very well.' Battabeng nodded. 'It is done.'

Juni's mouth gaped. 'Well, I suppose I could do it,' said the princess, shaking her head. 'It would of course be an honour, but I can't accept, either.'

'Why ever not?' asked the bemused Emperor. 'Is it such horrible thing to be leader of famous Guild?'

Juni turned to look at her crew. Thrugg's eyes were watery. Nephora was looking away but her blue skin, as usual, gave away her true feelings. Even the greedy little Quilch looked forlorn.

'I can't leave my crew behind,' she said.

The Emperor heaved with laughter. 'Then why not bring crew with you? For their bravery and service to peace in the Galaxy, Battabeng excuse all pirates and make all Night Eaters, if they wish it.'

Juni's eyes widened and she turned to her rag-tag crew.

'Well?' she asked. 'What do you think?'

Thrugg's expression lit up in an instant.

'Thrugg go with Juni always,' said the gladiator.

Nephora tried to play it cool, but her skin immediately flushed bright yellow. Juni grinned as she saw the Ureyan's skin and Nephora just shrugged.

'Looks like I'm in,' she said with a smile.

Finally, Quilch twittered and Juni couldn't help but laugh.

'Yes, Quilch,' she replied. 'Night Eaters are paid a salary.'

The Quilkin twittered excitedly and gave a feathery salute. Juni turned back to the Emperor.

'Looks like we're in.'

'Great,' said Speck, but he couldn't get any further, for he suddenly found himself within the princess's embrace.

'Thank you, Speck,' she said. 'For everything. But what are you going to do?'

'I think I'm about ready to go back to the Library,' he said thoughtfully. He looked from the brave princess to the regal Emperor. He looked up at the wise Vargel Pren, and then across to the diligent Nuis who had saved his life on so many occasions. Finally, he looked down to the little utility bots sitting next to him. M-T was still brimming with pride. Speck extended his hand and the little utility bot took hold of it with a claw.

My family, he thought with a smile.

'Yes,' he said at long last. 'I think I'm ready to go home.'

More great reading from Ford Street Publishing

50 GOOD REASONS TO READ
TRUST ME!

JUSTIN D'ATH
SALLY ODGERS
ROBERT HOOD
DEBORAH ABELA
LUCY SUSSEX
BILL CONDON
DIANNE BATES
CORAL TULLOCH
HAZEL EDWARDS
ALLAN BAILLIE
KEITH TAYLOR
JENNY BLACKFORD
MICHAEL PRYOR
SEAN MCMULLEN
GEORGE IVANOFF
CAROL JONES
DAVID RISH
JIM SCHEMBRI
SIMON HIGGINS
MEREDITH COSTAIN
KERRY GREENWOOD
RICHARD HARLAND
SOPHIE MASSON

LILI WILKINSON
SALLY RIPPIN
SCOT GARDNER
JENNY MOUNFIELD
KATE FORSYTH
SUE BURSZTYNSKI
GARY CREW
MARC MCBRIDE
ANDY GRIFFITHS
PHILLIP GWYNNE
JANET FINDLAY
LOUISE PROUT
DAVID METZENTHEN
DAVID MILLER
STEVEN HERRICK
MITCH VANE

DOUG MACLEOD
JAMES ROY
SHERRYL CLARK
MICHAEL WAGNER
SOFIE LAGUNA
CATHERINE BATESON
MEME MCDONALD
SHAUN TAN
LEIGH HOBBS
GRANT GITTUS
ISOBELLE CARMODY

Edited by Paul Collins

Introduction by ISOBELLE CARMODY

www.fordstreetpublishing.com

FORD ST

More great reading from Ford Street Publishing

CHEREE PETERS
TIME CATCHER

In a post-apocalyptic world of rigid rules, Althea's luxurious life is turned upside-down when she is kidnapped by the dreaded Variants. Betrayed by those she trusts most, Althea is forced to question everything she thought she knew – including who she is and what she's capable of.

Are the Variants dangerous insurgents or a new breed of human, fighting for freedom?

Althea must separate deception from truth to claim her own power.

Time Catcher is the first book in a trilogy by an exciting new voice in Australian fiction.

www.fordstreetpublishing.com   FORD ST